Grimhunters: The Curse of Roarke Lake

Kobi Madsen

Copyright

ISBN 978-0-9990295-3-4

Written by Kobi Madsen

Published by Amber Light Publishing
www.AmberLightPublishing.com

Editing and Interior Design by Nita Robinson
Nita Helping Hand?
www.NitaHelpingHand.com

DEDICATION

For Ana Pires,

My amazing teacher and counsellor. Thank you for always believing in me. It is you who inspired me to commit to it fully. Thank you for supporting and guiding me throughout my journey.

For my sister, Kendra,

Thank you for always believing in me and for cheering me on through the hard times and the good times. I am so thankful for your continuous support and your never-ending patience.

Contents

Chapter One

March 24, 1988 – A boy named Victor, along with his family, moved into a house on a lake close to a town called Roarke. Victor and his family moved from Seattle because his father, David, bought a small business in town called Snider's Cuts and planned to be the manager. He later renamed it Hyde's Cuts.

On arrival to their house, they unloaded their luggage and furniture. Victor and his sister, Natalie, instantly searched for their bedrooms. Natalie shouted first, "I call that room!" spotting her favorite.

Victor asked, "Why do you get that room?"

"Well, because I'm the oldest and I'm a girl so I get the bigger room."

Victor's mom joined the conversation asking, "Why are you two arguing?"

"Mom, why does she get this room?" asked Victor. "I wanted this room; it's not fair." Arguing with his sister was annoying and she always called him a "snap show" because of how angry he got. This made him even angrier because she seemed to know this would set him off.

His mom, Susan, replied, "It doesn't matter what room you get, just find another and bring your things inside." Victor walked away, down the hallway and found another room that had a window above the bed and enough room for a dresser drawer, a study table and perhaps a television set.

Victor knew that it was usually Natalie that started the fights and that she was the real "snap show" since she was always so negative with everyone. Natalie thought she could tell anyone what to do, even her own parents. She was pretty much known for being a big mouth and was happy when her dad said that they would be moving away. A new start meant she could avoid everyone she knew back in Seattle who knew her personality and hated her because of it. If day one was any indication, she was off to the same start in Roarke.

Victor's dad called everyone to come down and help bring the mattresses up to the rooms, "Alright, I'll grab the top and Victor, you grab the bottom as we tilt the sides upward so they'll fit through. Susan and Natalie, you grab the other bed." They lifted it, which wasn't easy as it was quite heavy, at times hitting the side walls as they walked, but in the end they finally made it upstairs. They brought one into

Natalie's room and one into Victor's. David and Victor went back downstairs to grab the bigger bed for the master bedroom that his mother and father would occupy. They carried it upstairs, which took what seemed like twice the time the other beds took. This particular bed was massive compared to the others, making him forget about his earlier complaints. This had been the real hard work. Susan and Natalie were upstairs ready to help them squeeze it into their parents' room, and finally the worst was over. From there everyone brought their belongings inside to their rooms and life in Roarke began.

The day had been hard. They were tired and their muscles ached. Trying to rush wouldn't have been an option given the narrow hallways and corners. Victor had been nervous, which was normal for times like this. He often felt afraid that he would mess up and not be able to handle things. He worried that people would call him a wimp. At times he'd felt like dropping the furniture as the weight was too much, but didn't as he refused to show any sort of weakness. He fought off the pain until they had finished the move, making sure his father couldn't single him out. Everything that had already happened that day had him starting to wish that he was somewhere else, even for just a moment. Somewhere that his dad and sister wouldn't see him, giving him a short release and time to reset his mind.

The bulk of the rooms were filled, yet Victor's mom continued to stress over where she wanted the different pieces of furniture to be placed. David said, "The T.V. would look good in front of the window, the couch can be across from the window facing the T.V., the table can be between the couch and the T.V., and the carpet under the table." He hoped that giving these suggestions would help make his wife happy since so much was going on in her head. Susan struggled to picture how the room would look if they did what David suggested. She wanted to do it right the first time but it was becoming clear that her paranoia might get in the way. Time would tell when their new house would finally become a home.

David was annoyed at how sensitive his wife seemed to be about this move. It reminded him of why he wanted to start all over, leaving the stress and problems of Seattle behind. Maybe in his desire to leave Seattle, David may have forgotten to fully consider how his family felt about the move deep down inside, even though they seemed fine with it on the outside. On the face of it, the family appeared content, but their reactions on the first day may have shown something else.

Susan did settle down shortly saying, "That's actually not a bad idea, thanks, hon."

After unpacking, Victor took a walk down to see

the lakeshore and get a breath of fresh air. He stared out across the lake and wondered if their house was the only house at the lake since no others were obvious to him. He picked up a flat rock and threw it at the water, hoping to watch it skip like they do on T.V. After the rock made the first splash, it didn't skip. He gave up and began to walk back to the house. When he arrived, he heard a twig break in the forest to his left. This startled Victor as it could have been anything.

He called out, "Hello, is anyone there?" but there was no response. Once again he heard more twigs break, causing him to get really scared and take three big steps backward as a man appeared out of the woods. Victor let his breath out loudly, realizing he had been holding his breath from being scared. He managed to focus for a second, looking at this stranger and said, "Hi, my name is Victor. What's your name?"

The man didn't hesitate in responding, "My name is Willy, though some call me Willy the Hillbilly."

Victor could see why, given his appearance. He was probably the scruffiest man he had ever seen. His clothes looked torn and he smelled. Victor also began to hope that the man wouldn't offer him beer or a cigarette because he didn't know if he'd have the confidence to say no. Victor was always shy, even when he would say hi to people he knew, he would remain shy. But he managed to put a smile on his face and be as approachable as possible. The man had a somewhat angry voice, but he seemed friendly enough to Victor.

Willy asked, "Did you just move into this house?"

Victor replied, "Yes, we moved here from Seattle."

"Really, I hear you city kids are real punks," said Willy rudely.

"Oh no, that's not true. My friends and I are very mature. There was one guy that was kind of loud, though he was alright."

Victor's face turned red as Willy pressed on asking, "You mean your friends from Seattle?"

"Yes, of course. I haven't had time to make any friends here yet," said Victor with a discouraged tone to his voice. It had already crossed Victor's mind that making new friends in his new home might be difficult.

Willy asked, "Well, what's wrong?"

In an odd way Victor was comfortable opening up

to this stranger and replied, "I miss the city and my friends."

Willy began to get the feeling that he was getting too personal and decided to get off the topic to make Victor feel better. Willy walked closer to Victor and asked, "How come your family moved here anyway?"

"Well, because my father bought a business. He manages a barber shop in town," Victor answered. "My father was a salesman in Seattle but ever since high school he's wanted to be a barber. So after he made enough money, he bought a business in this town."

"Which barber shop is it, because there's at least two or three in town?"

"It's called Sni...,"

"Hey Victor," said David, walking outside the house and interrupting the conversation. "Who's your new friend?"

Victor replied, "Dad, this is Willy. We just met a few minutes ago."

David said to Willy, "Hi, my name is David. Nice to meet you. I see you've met my son, Victor. Maybe I should introduce you to the rest of the family." He called out to Susan and Natalie, "Hey Susan, Natalie get out here. There's someone I want you to meet."

As they came out, interested in seeing who the man was, Susan asked, "Who's this?"

"This is Willy. Willy, this is my wife, Susan, and my daughter, Natalie."

Willy gave them a curt nod and said, "Nice to meet you. We were just talking about your move here."

David said, "Oh yeah, just needed to get away from things." Both Susan and Natalie looked at him with confusion as he changed the subject by saying, "Did you want to stay for dinner?" Susan wasn't impressed and poked him from behind.

Willy shouted cheerfully, "Yes, I love eating good food around the dinner table!" Willy had said it like he hadn't been given an offer like that for a long time, appreciating the gesture.

"Great, come on in," said David, putting his arm around Willy's shoulder as they walked toward the house, "You're going to love my wife's cooking."

Susan was mad at David and could not believe he would actually invite a homeless man into their home. They didn't really know if he was homeless; he could've had a house on the lake, but Susan made an assumption based on what she saw. She just couldn't understand how he could hand out an invitation to someone they didn't know after just moving in, especially when he smelled so bad. David was a fair man, but sometimes he took things just a little too far. Victor was much like his father in this way, which is probably what kept the conversation going when he first met Willy.

Natalie was thinking the same thing Susan was and didn't feel comfortable around Willy. This brought to mind the expression, 'like father, like son', but in this case for her and Susan it was, 'like mother, like daughter'. Natalie whispered to her mom, "This guy looks like a total bum."

Victor overheard and whispered back, "Oh, leave him alone. Besides, he might not be staying that long."

Susan marched into the kitchen to find a chair and speak to David while everyone went into the dining room. "Why did you invite him in?" she asked.

"The man looks hungry and like he needs help, so can you please just be nice?" David scolded.

"I think there's more to it than that. You looked

like you didn't want to speak about the part of our move here."

David replied, "It's got nothing to do with that. I mean, if it was a child and he or she was hungry, would you let them starve?"

"That's a child, this is a grown man."

"You have got to help the homeless once in a while."

Susan still didn't believe it and replied, "Well, at least wash your hands and arms before dinner."

"Why should I wash both of my arms? I only put one arm around him."

"Well, I want to make sure you're really clean before dinner."

After they were finished talking, Susan went into the room and took a seat. They were all waiting for dinner, and when David brought the turkey in, the delicious aroma took over, taking the focus off Willy's smell. David started carving and giving pieces to each person around the table. It looked like a delicious turkey and they were all excited to eat. This was actually the first time Victor ate turkey because he had always been a very picky guy. Although he had always been consistent about the things he ate, with a new town and home he was willing to try something new. This really surprised everyone as Victor could be pretty stubborn when it came to things like that.

David turned to Willy and asked, "Hey, do you like it?"

"It's the best food I've had in twelve years."

"Well, I told you that you would like my wife's cooking," as they ate through dinner.

Susan asked, "So Willy, where do you live?"

"I live a mile down the lake."

Victor asked, "How big is this lake?"

"Well, I would say it goes for four to six miles."

Victor could not believe that Willy told him it went that far. He made a little motion with his face saying, "Really? That's far."

"Of course, being known as the lake hermit, I've been the only one who has lived at and who has wanted to visit this lake for a long time."

"Really interesting. So why is that?"

"Well, back then, before my grandfather was even born, this was a great place to come to in the summer, but not anymore. You see, I'm fifty-seven years old and people think I'm crazy to still be here."

Victor asked, "So there really isn't anyone else that lives on this lake?"

Willy was nervous when Victor asked him that question and looked down answering suspiciously, "No," as he stood up, thanking them for dinner and saying goodbye.

Before anyone could respond, the door slammed and Willy was gone. Something in what Victor had asked Willy made him nervous enough to speed walk to point of nearly running out the door. It was obvious that Willy knew something sinister that he didn't think they should know about. This made everyone uncomfortable and curious as to what Victor could have said to scare him off. The look on Willy's face only added to the suspense. Was it the question that was asked or was it the answer he didn't want to give?

Victor was looking forward to tomorrow on the off chance he might see Willy and get a chance to ask him why he'd been in such a rush to leave that night. The family finished eating and chatted about Willy's reaction, throwing around all sorts of possibilities and adding more fuel to the fire. Everybody brought their dishes to the sink and Victor offered to wash them, giving his mom a break. Four hours later the sun went down and his parents told Victor and Natalie to go to bed in preparation for the big day tomorrow.

The two of them headed upstairs as Victor said to Natalie, "They don't have to tell me to go to bed, I'm sixteen years old."

Natalie, being the older one said, "Well, I need my sleep to wake up in the morning and go into town to look for work, you need it for your first day at school. If you don't change your attitude, a job is something I'm sure you'll never have, just like your buddy, Willy."

Victor did not like being criticized by his sister and began to bubble. Natalie always seemed to know how to push his buttons and it didn't matter what it was about. Victor would always try to convince her that she was wrong. Just as it wasn't right to judge someone based on appearance, Natalie continued to portray herself as the victim when, in Victor's opinion, she continued to be one with too much sarcasm.

Natalie walked to her room and said, "Whatever, I'm going to bed."

Victor followed, looking forward to falling asleep. This didn't go as planned for Victor, which wasn't unusual for him. Victor stayed up for half an hour doodling on the wall before dozing off.

Before long, Victor was awakened to the sound of a loud howl. His eyes flew open wide and he got up to look out the window. He was curious as to what had made that howl. Late at night was a good time for any predator to hunt since they could use the darkness to their advantage when they stalked their prey. Victor's curiosity was soon overtaken by his fatigue and he ended up back in bed. He told himself how lucky he was to be inside his house, safe from the scary things that go bump in the night. Victor slept until dawn.

Meanwhile, sometime around 10:00 p.m., a man named Hugo was driving out past the lake to pick up the drugs he had smuggled and hidden from the authorities, which was somewhere in the bushes. He had a gun with him for protection as, of course, it was part of his job to have one. As he parked the car near the trees, he went to search for his hiding place. He had buried the container that held the drugs about two feet in the ground. After about ten minutes had gone by, he managed to retrieve it and just wanted to get it to his superiors fast.

When he carried the supplies to his car, he found his vehicle had been turned upside down. Hugo was furious and confused at the same time. He decided to re-bury the container to avoid the risk of being caught by patrol men, so the only way he could bring the drugs into town without being caught was to bring back another vehicle.

After re-burying the container, he desperately wanted to take his anger out on something so he shot an owl that was sitting on a tree branch above his head. He had seen that same owl other nights when he had made runs. Before, it had always seemed like music to his ears, but this time he couldn't have cared less and shot it down.

As he walked away, with his hand still gripping the gun, he heard noises in the trees. He thought about investigating what had made the noise, but he just continued walking. He then heard it again, only this time he decided to do some further investigation. Believing that someone may have followed him, he put both hands on the gun and pointed it out at the surrounding trees. He slowly moved around to where the noise came from, then ducked down behind a tree.

He shouted, "Look, whoever's out there, show yourself! I have a gun!" Suddenly he heard noises behind him, then in front of him. He began pointing the gun back and forth really quickly, then, after seeing nothing he finally said, "Forget this, I'm out of here." As he ran back to where his car was, he heard something approaching from behind. He hid behind the trunk of the car with his hands still tightly gripping the gun. As he crouched down even lower, he could see through the windows of the upside down car. Suddenly, hairy feet with claws appeared, though unlike any animal he had seen since it was standing on two legs. He popped up to fire his gun and, although lightning fast, the creature was nowhere to be seen. Hugo turned around to run, but when he did, the creature was there, up close, and took a powerful swing at Hugo, tearing his head off as he fell dead.

Chapter Two

It was now morning and time to get up for school. Victor was terrible at getting up early by himself so he relied on his mother who would yell upstairs, causing him to jump out of his bed. "Victor, it's time to get up!"

Victor jumped saying, "Huh, oh ok, I'm coming!" Victor got out of his bed, still tired, and walked downstairs. His mother already had breakfast ready for him. Since Victor was really picky about the things he ate, he would eat the same things for breakfast every day. He would also eat the same things for lunch and dinner each day. For breakfast he would have cereal, for lunch a hotdog with ketchup, cookies and fruit, and for dinner he would eat eggs and bacon. Victor loved all of these foods and had a hard time resisting them, but he just wouldn't try anything else.

After he finished eating, he went upstairs to get a shower, get dressed, brush his teeth and put on deodorant. Victor had his daily routines; they had become a habit that he would not miss for years to come.

Victor was nervous about going to the new school and was starting to wish his family had never moved here. He wanted to tell his dad how he felt, but he didn't want to let him down.

It took twelve minutes to drive from the lake into town, which meant Victor had to leave a little earlier to get there on time. It always felt easier when the rest of his family wasn't at the house in the mornings. It was more peaceful, knowing it was just him and his mom. Victor always liked to watch T.V. in the living room while his mom was in the kitchen making his breakfast.

His mother handed him his books for school and asked him to get in the car. "Victor, are you ready? Let's go now."

When they drove away Victor asked, "Mom, did you hear howls last night?"

His mother said, "No, I was asleep."

"I heard them and didn't exactly go to sleep when you told me to."

"Victor, you have to be in bed early so you don't feel tired for school."

"Yeah but Mom, it's embarrassing when you tell

me to do that when I'm sixteen years old. I'm a senior in high school."

"You're not. You're in grade ten. You're just a sophomore..."

As they drove down the road and were about to come into town, they saw a man walking on the side of the road. It was Willy and it looked like he was heading into town. Victor didn't know how Willy could just go into town looking the way he did. Victor didn't know Willy's past, but nobody's life starts out like the one Willy had now. Willy seemed like a very unhappy guy since he never smiled, and last night sure didn't help. Victor wanted to know more about him and wanted to know why he was in such a rush to leave last night. Perhaps after school he would try to find out where he lived in the woods. The only clue that Willy did say was that he lived on the lake, a mile down, wherever that was.

It looked like Willy was carrying a bag by the way he was walking with his back bent over. Victor tried to wave at him out the window, but Willy didn't see him in time. Susan asked, "Who was that you were waving at?"

Not thinking she cared, Victor said, "No one."

"Well, it must have been no one since we just

moved into a new town just yesterday. So who was it?"

"It was Willy."

"Why would you wave at him?"

"Why not? He is a good man."

"We don't know that, he could be dangerous."

Victor and his mom didn't speak again until just before they got to school. He asked, "When did dad leave this morning?"

"He left at 5:00 a.m. to go to the shop," said Susan, smiling. "It's going to be great here, don't you think?"

Victor looked out the window, sadly responding, "Yeah, sure."

His mother looked at him after hearing the tone of his voice and asked, "What's wrong, Victor?"

"I miss Seattle and my friends."

At that moment they arrived at school. As Victor got out of the car, Susan said, "Victor, I know moving is not easy, but give it a chance and you might like it here. To begin, you should try to make friends at school."

After that, both of them said, "Goodbye." Victor went into the school to find the principal's office. When he did, he spoke to the secretary. "Hi, I'm here to see the principal."

She brought him into the office to meet the principal and when she did, Victor introduced himself. He showed the principal his timetable and what class he had first. The principal said, "Well Victor, I'm Principal Sal Mooney and I would be happy to show you where your first class is."

After he took him to his first class, he explained to Victor that he would then have a starting point, and from there he could make his way to his other classes.

The schedule read that Victor had Social Studies first, but he didn't know whose class he was in. There were two of them for his grade, so the principal took him there, already having a good idea where Victor had been placed and which classes he was enrolled in. He ended up having to be in Ms. Martin's class since she taught grade ten Socials. He knew that Victor would like her class since she was probably the easiest teacher in the school. She even let students correct their own quizzes before handing them in after she went over it with them.

The principal knocked on the door and Ms. Martin said, "Hi, Principal M. What can I do for you?"

"Ms. Martin, this is your new student."

"What's his name?"

"His name is Victor Hyde."

After the principal spoke to Ms. Martin, he left and the teacher assigned Victor a seat. She asked, "So Victor, where did you move from and where are you living now?"

"My family and I moved here from Seattle because my dad bought a barber shop here in town that he wants to manage. We live in a house down by the lake." After hearing Victor's story, everyone started looking at each other, whispering. Even the teacher looked puzzled.

Victor wondered why everyone began chatting right after he said where he lived, but finally the teacher said, "Well, I'm sure it's a nice place to live. Anyway, we were learning about the War of 1812 between Britain and France. I'll get you a text book," she said, changing the subject. "Now Steven, what happened in lower and upper Canada when the war occurred?"

Steven answered nervously, "In Upper Canada people fought the British, and in Lower Canada people were loyal British subjects." The teacher had a rather strict and disappointed look on her face since she believed Steven should have known the correct answer by now. Sometimes Steven would stay after school to get help from her since Socials wasn't his best subject.

Hamilton, the person sitting next to Steven, tried to quickly whisper to Steven what the correct answer was, although the teacher went ahead and said, "Sorry, that's wrong. In Upper Canada they fought as loyal British subjects, and in Lower Canada people fought defending their homes. It's not that hard to remember when you study." The look on Steven's face showed that he was embarrassed. He didn't like being picked, fearing he would get the answer wrong.

The teacher gave them worksheets for the chapter. "By the end of the block I want you all to get this work done." The entire class was whining, questioning her about the work and she responded, "By the end of the block!"

Hamilton reached over Steven's shoulder, "That was really amazing, Steven," said Hamilton sarcastically.

"How about you go and play that French horn of

yours since you've got a lot of energy to speak to me like that."

"Hmm, maybe I should to help the class work. Seriously though, why can't you work harder to learn this shit?"

"Are you done so I can work now?"

"Yeah sure, I'm done. By the way, the new kid. Did he say his name was Victor?" asked Hamilton.

"I guess so, why?"

"Well, maybe I should move over to his side to sit next to him since I can't deal with you anymore."

"Go ahead, I'm fine," said Steven nonchalantly.

Hamilton got out of his seat and went over to sit in the seat next to Victor. Hamilton said, "Hi, do you mind if I sit next to you?"

"Uh sure, my name's Victor."

"I'm Hamilton, but people call me Ham for short."

"Well, it's nice to meet you, Ham. So what made you want to move over here?"

Ham pointed out saying, "You see the guy over there?"

Victor responded, "Yes."

"Well, his name is Steven. He's kind of bad in this class and I just can't work with him right now."

"Does the teacher mind you moving over here?"

"Oh no, just as long as you don't cause any trouble, it's fine. And right now it'd just be best for Steven to work by himself."

As they worked on their assignments, Victor was getting his work done quickly, and in a matter of ten minutes he was close to being done. After about twenty minutes the teacher asked them to hand in their papers. Victor was done and so were a few others, but a few weren't and had to take it for homework. Soon after, the bell sounded and Victor was walking down the hallway to his next class. Ham walked with him and enviously said, "Wow, you really went for it back there."

"Thanks. I mean, I love history, it's like reading a book."

"Ha, yeah and most people think history is a waste .

of time because they don't believe it has any impact on their lives."

"Well Ham, the more you know about the past, the more prepared you are for the future."

"That's true. Well, I'm going to head down to class, so I guess I'll see you later?"

"Yeah sure, see you then."

"Bye," they both said as they went their separate ways.

Steven, however, caught up to Victor and said, "Hi, I'm Steven."

Then Victor said, "Hi, I'm Victor."

"Which class are you going to?"

"I have Cooking, what about you?" asked Victor.

"I have the same!" said Steven with excitement in his voice. "Is it true that you live out on the lake?"

Victor looked at him, thinking of that moment in Socials class when everyone was surprised. "Yes, why do you ask?"

Steven said nothing at first, but then responded, "Oh nothing, I was just curious."

"Ham told me about you back there."

"And what did he say?" asked Steven angrily.

"Not too much. He mentioned that you don't care too much for Socials."

"Yeah well, I could care less about that class."

"Ha, ha yeah, Ham and I were just talking about that," said Victor with amusement.

They came to their cooking class and Victor went to the teacher to tell her that he was a new student in her class. Her name was Ms. Unger and she was beautiful and much younger than Ms. Martin. She was trying to assign Victor to a group when Steven asked if he could be in his group. She appeared fine with it and Victor went with Steven to his cooking group. Ms. Unger said, "Okay class, today we shall be making muffins, so get out your recipe and come up here to get your ingredients."

Steven introduced Victor to the others in the group, Ned and Jared. They got out their tray so one of them could go up to the teacher and get their ingredients. Victor didn't have good social skills so he remained silent most of the time while his group worked. When people were talking, he didn't know how to engage in the conversation and make it sound interesting. Back in Seattle, people always thought of Victor as annoying when he talked. Victor could see their point but he also knew he was trying to be friendly. So now he would take it slow and let others talk to him first.

They got out all the plates and custard cups. After seeing the two go up, one following and helping the other, Victor asked Steven again, "Why were you curious about me living at the lake? I really want to know."

"Well, have you heard about the area around the lake?"

Victor replied, "No."

Then Steven answered back, "It's dangerous."

"Why is it dangerous?"

"Nobody knows, but for years people have gone missing."

Victor asked with fear in his voice, "Missing... what do you mean missing?"

"The police didn't find any evidence." Ned and Jared came back with the ingredients and began to bake. Victor was very puzzled about what Steven told him and planned to tell his parents.

Ned shouted, "Hey guys, I hear someone was arrested today."

Steven asked, "Who?"

"You know that man, Hugh, the one who moved here four years ago with his son, Hugo?"

"Yeah, the junkie and the dropout?"

Victor asked him, "Wait, who are these guys?"

Steven answered, "Well, four years ago a man named Hugh and his son, Hugo, moved from Indiana to here. They always seemed weird. As it turns out they are both thieves and have been charged for over six felonies."

"So what was it this time?" asked Victor.

Jared replied, "Well the dad, Hugh, has been arrested for drug smuggling."

"What about the son?" asked Steven.

"They found the son sometime this morning somewhere around the lake with his head decapitated. They also found Hugo's own little stash of drugs and his car flipped upside down. No one knows who or what attacked him, but his dad and their boss from out of town have been arrested after they found evidence in the car at the crime scene. In the end, it took a confession from someone about the drugs to get the arrest.

At the end of the block, Victor went to his next class, which happened to be English. Victor hated reading immensely, and once again he had to introduce himself and get a seat. His teacher greeted him, handed him a book and showed Victor to his desk, giving Victor a brief description of what they'd be reading to get him caught up. They were starting where they left off from yesterday, on page 57. It was The Chrysalids, a book about mutants that were treated as outcasts. As the class got started reading where they'd left off, Victor joined in.

They read silently for twenty minutes at which point the teacher gave them a worksheet with fifteen questions to complete during the rest of class. Victor was a slow reader and always felt he would have to read things multiple times to understand it and knew he would have to do it as homework.

Victor enjoyed non-fiction rather than fiction. At

the end of the block the teacher told his students that he wanted them to study the chapter for homework as there would be a quiz tomorrow.

Victor headed to his last class, which was Photography. This was another thing that Victor enjoyed and happened to be very good at. People back in Seattle had always told him that he was good at taking pictures, and it usually meant he was given the camera at family functions.

He walked through the classroom door for another round of introductions. Victor was getting tired of all the intros and the nervous tension he felt meeting new people. He sat down, and the teacher gave them an assignment to take photos this week and put them on the cardboard posters each of them had been given. There Victor saw Ham again. "Hey, Victor!" said Ham cheerfully.

"Hey Ham, surprised to see you here."

"I know, right. So, do you have a partner?"

"No, after all I just got here."

"Well, I could join up with you since we met earlier," Ham offered.

"Yeah sure, that makes it easy." They sat down

while Ham showed him his camera and Victor said, "So, I met Steven today. We walked down the hall together and have Cooking together. I'm in his group. He sure seemed nice."

"Yeah, he means well," said Ham.

"So you don't have another partner in this class?"

"No. Well I did, though not anymore."

"What happened to him?"

Ham pointed saying, "You see that boy close to the teacher's desk?"

"Yeah," answered Victor.

"He was my partner. His name is Keller Reid. Don't get me started on him."

"Why, what did he do?"

"Let's just say I'd rather be partners with Steven than with him, if he was here. That is, of course, if you weren't here and he was the only other choice. The thing is, that guy Keller is weird. He's kind of eerie, especially since he likes to keep to himself all the time, so I just decided to work alone until you showed up."

"Well, I don't have to ask anything else about it if you don't want."

"It's alright. So, did you have Cooking last?"

"No, I had Cooking after Socials and then English."

"Oh yeah, I had Art and then Band after Socials. Keller is in my art class. He's actually really good."

"And how about Band, what do you play?" asked Victor.

"I play the French horn."

"Wow, I wish I could play an instrument."

"Steven was teasing me in Socials to play for the class. I thought him disappointing the teacher because he still wasn't doing so good was the reason she had been so strict with us. That's the first time…"

"Well, I'm not perfect since in Cooking I let my group do all the work and I just followed. English, well, I like reading history more than fiction books."

"Well, it's good to know Steven can be helpful."

Near the end of school, Ham asked Victor if he

wanted to hang out with him and Steven after school. Despite their differences in school, Ham would hang out with Steven each day. As soon as the bell rang they walked outside the front door of the school and waited for Steven to show. Once he did he said, "Oh, hi Victor. You hanging out with us?"

Victor looked over to Steven and said, "Yeah, Ham invited me. So where are we going?"

Steven replied, "Ollie's."

"What's Ollie's?" asked Victor, grinning.

Ham answered, "It's a corner store close to a skate park, just straight ahead from the high school. It's also right next to a Pro Fitness gym."

They started walking and about six minutes later, they arrived at Ollie's. Ham said, "We can have a seat inside, they have five booths."

"Wow, it's actually quite big for a corner store," said Victor with astonishment. They went inside and took a seat close to the door.

Ham offered, "I'll buy. What do you guys want?"

Steven answered, "I'll take a French Vanilla."

Ham turned to Victor and asked, "What do you want, Victor?"

"Oh, I'm fine."

"C'mon, I offered to pay!"

"No... really, I'm fine!" said Victor refusing again.

"There must be something you want, because I really do want to get it for you."

"Well, do they have slushies?" asked Victor.

"Yes," replied Ham.

"Alright, I'll take a cherry if they have one."

"On it."

As Ham went to the counter to get the drinks, someone else walked in from the field with his soccer ball to get himself something. There were two clerks. Ham was dealing with one, while the boy went to the other on Ham's left side. The boy said, "Hey, Hamilton."

"Hey, Danny."

The boy's order was faster than Ham's and as the

clerk brought it over she said, "Here you go, Danny. Have a nice day."

"Sure, take care."

A moment later, Ham brought the drinks over to Steven and Victor and they both said, "Thanks."

"You're welcome!" said Ham.

After he sat down, Victor asked, "So, who was that guy?"

Ham replied, "Just another friend…"

"What's his name?"

"His name is Danny and he's Mr. Mooney's least favorite kid in school."

"Interesting, why is that?"

"When we were ten we were in a go-cart derby at this carnival that comes to town every spring. During the race, he was beating almost everyone until he finally came in second place, about to take first.

He started driving so recklessly that when they came to a turn, he lost control and hit the person in front hard on his right. At that point when he tried to stop, he went off the track. He tried to get out of the way and when he was about to hit someone he turned around her fast. He pulled on the wheel again, making him go into a 360 degree spin as he was still moving forward fast. Finally, he got a hold of himself and was driving straight again, but the last step was when he finally crashed into someone else. And that was Principal Mooney. He hit his ankle, causing him to trip and fall, then his drink was spilt all over his shirt. Principal Mooney stayed on crutches for three weeks," explained Steven thoroughly.

"So, why didn't he just stop after all those unexpected events?" asked Victor.

"He said he was just having fun. He tried to stop when he saw Principal Mooney, although he said he was going too fast, was too close, and that it was too late. Since then, he's tried not to get into trouble with the Principal since we got to high school, fearing he'd give him shit."

"That's quite a story!" said Victor.

Then Ham spoke, "Yeah, Steven and I were in between it at the race, causing everyone to crash into each other. What an ugly mess it was, but don't worry, no one on the track was hurt."

Victor was relieved to hear that and replied, "Well,

that's great to hear!"

As they continued drinking, Victor saw Willy outside the store window and said, "I know that guy. He lives on the lake too."

Steven laughed, "What, him? Ha! Ha! Ha!"

Victor asked, "You know him?"

"Yeah, he's the lake hermit, Willy the Hillbilly!"

"Yes, I've heard. He told me that's what people call him. Is Willy a country person?"

"No, he just seems like it, especially since he lost his dad years ago."

"What happened to him?" asked Victor.

"He had a heart attack... After that Willy went crazy and started to turn into a bum. Wait, did you speak to him?" asked Steven.

"Yes, and we had dinner with him at my house."

Steven laughed again, "Ha! Ha! Ha!"

Victor was feeling irritated with Steven and said,

"Well, I should probably go. My house is a ways from here."

"Alright, we'll see you at school tomorrow," said Ham.

"Yeah, sure, see you tomorrow. Maybe…" said Victor muttering.

After walking outside, Victor ran up to Willy and said, "Hi, Willy. How's your day been?"

Willy looked over his right shoulder, feeling disconcerted. He responded, "Fine, and you look like you started school?"

"Yes I did, and for my first day, it actually wasn't bad. My classes are great and I met two kids around my age. One seems to be my friend right now, and the other not so sure yet. Their names are Ham and Steven. Steven called you that name you said people call you around here, but I didn't like and decided to take off."

As they walked from the town back to the lake, which was probably six miles, Victor wanted to know why Willy came to town and what was in his bag.

"Willy, did you see my mom and I drive by you this morning?"

"No, although I thought I saw someone waving at me from a car window."

"Yes, that was me! How come you came to town today?"

Willy answered, "Oh, I just came to get out. I don't get out of the house much."

"What's in the bag?"

"Just supplies I got from the hardware store."

"Supplies for what?"

Willy was silent for a few seconds and said, "These are just tools for working on my house. My house is kind of a shack and always needs repairs."

Victor believed him at first, but then Willy's old worn out bag ripped open in the back and the stuff inside fell out onto the ground. There were tools that fell out, but also sticks of dynamite. Victor could see that Willy was telling the truth, but not completely.

Victor asked, "Why do you have dynamite in your bag?"

Willy appeared very jumpy and replied, "Oh this? It's just for an experiment." Victor was suspicious and pushed on by asking him what Steven asked him earlier.

"Willy, do you know anything about this lake that you're not telling me, something that has to do with people disappearing?"

"Disappearances at the lake?" asked Willy with dissimulation.

"Well, this morning at school when I told people where I was living they seemed surprised, and Steven also told me about this."

As they came closer to the lake Willy said, "Be careful Victor, and don't go anywhere else down the lake."

"What do you mean by that?" Willy ran into the woods and Victor yelled, "Willy!"

Willy didn't look back to respond, and Victor went along home.

Victor opened the door as his dad welcomed him, "Hi Victor, all done for the day, huh? How was school today?"

Victor walked upstairs, "School was great, and I did make friends, before you ask."

His father said, "Well that's great, I'm happy for you."

Victor went into his room, still a little freaked out, and got started on his homework and studying for the quiz in English. Later on, the family gathered to eat dinner. As they ate, Susan asked Natalie how her job interview had gone.

"It was great, and I feel like I would have loved being a bank accountant in Seattle."

David answered, "Very funny Natalie, and I must say my business is going well. I'm still trying to get to know people, but so far it's good. What about you Victor, how did your classes go today?"

"Oh I'm... it was great. Hey, Mom and Dad, did you hear about this lake?"

David asked, "What about it, Victor?"

"Well, a friend of mine at school said that people have gone missing here, and then after school I walked back home with Willy and he seemed like he knew something too."

Susan said, "You shouldn't listen to what that hermit tells you. It's not something that we really need to talk about now. Let's just eat and talk about something else."

After they finished, Victor couldn't stop thinking about what he heard earlier that day, so he went upstairs to finish his homework and try to get his mind off it. Before long the sun was starting to set over the mountains and he took this as his signal to go to bed.

Victor always believed that even when you're a kid, life is hard. And they had problems too...

Before he got into bed, he heard more howls, except this time it sounded like more than one creature.

Victor had always been afraid of going outside into the dark more than anyone else because night was the best time for predators wanting to get the jump on people. He would usually just stay inside the house after dark. Even during the day he liked to be inside, especially when there was no school. He was not overly confident and had even convinced himself that he was afraid to go out in public sometimes. In spite of all that, he was somewhat happy that he'd done well on his first day in town.

The howling continued as Victor gazed out the window. It was dark and he couldn't see anything. It sounded so loud that it felt like they were close to his house. Victor left his bedroom to say goodnight to everyone.

"Goodnight Mom and Dad. Oh, and goodnight to you too, Natalie."

Everyone said goodnight to Victor, even Natalie, although her tone was very sarcastic. Victor made his way to bed, packing his books and setting his clothes out for the next day.

Chapter Three

The next morning, Victor woke up early without his mom's help. He ate breakfast and washed up for school. His mom awoke, surprised to see Victor up already.

"Mom, when can I get my driver's license?"

"When you're eighteen."

"But sixteen should be old enough."

"I don't care. I want you to get it when you're close to being an adult. When I was your age, I didn't want to get it until I was older."

"Well, can you at least pick me up from school every day? It's too far to walk from school to here."

"Well I could, although I can't promise anything since I won't always have the car."

Shortly after, Susan took Victor to school. When they arrived, he got out and said goodbye.

Victor wondered what pictures he could take by Friday for his photography class. There were, most likely, some interesting things at the lake that would be great for the project since he had heard people went missing there. He wondered what kind of stuff he might find as his imagination ran wild with the great possibilities, although the imagination can be a traumatic thing with no limits to where it can take you. His grandfather had once told him to use his imagination and the world would be a wonderful place to see. His grandparents, who lived in Denmark, were his father's parents. Victor and his family hadn't seen them for over six years, almost as long as he hadn't seen his cousins from his mom's side.

After his mom dropped him off at school, he ventured off inside to his cooking class. Steven was already there setting up for the meal they had to prepare, which was pasta. They said hi to each other as Victor sat down. Steven said, "Hey Victor, we were just talking about you. About where you live."

As they continued talking, the other two went off to get the ingredients. Victor replied, "So Steven, I spoke to Willy yesterday and he seemed really strange. Everyone here seems to know something about the lake, but Willy is just too secretive."

"That old man is a lunatic, you know, and I can't believe you've actually been talking to him."

"He's not a lunatic... Every time I speak to him, I can tell that he's probably one of the nicest guys I have ever met."

They began cooking. Near the end of class they sat down to taste their marvelous creation. Victor decided not to have any since he really didn't like to try new things.

Back in Seattle he had become known as the only kid who would never try anything new, and now his new classmates were going to learn that same little secret about him. After Cooking class he went to Socials class, which he could tell was going to be a long block. He was ahead of the game, and had already done the work she had assigned. This time, the person who sat next to him was Steven, and Ham seemed alright with it. Steven had told him that he wanted to sit with Victor today. Victor was uncomfortable, though he was grateful that Steven wanted to sit next to him.

After class Victor walked outside the door and down the hallway, when he accidently bumped into Keller Reid. Victor said, "Sorry," but after he did, Keller just looked at him with a very gloomy look and walked away. Victor continued his way to class and for the next two hours he had his other classes, English and Photography. At 3:10 p.m., the bell rang and he made his way outside.

Victor knew he'd done well on his quiz in English class, leaving him in a good mood as he and his mom drove home. When they arrived, Victor brought his backpack into the house and said, "Mom, I'm going for a walk in the woods. I'll be back later."

"Okay, but don't go too far."

Victor walked into the woods to see what was on the other side of the lake and to check out what Willy had told him about yesterday. As he walked through the forest, the path led him to the edge of the lake where the walking was easy. This was much better and he didn't get as dirty as he had walking in the mud and bushes. It looked like he was going to get to see all kinds of nature as the path led him in and out of the forest.

At some point he was on the beach and able to look back at the area where his house was. He couldn't believe how far he had travelled down the lake. It didn't seem like he had gone nearly that far, but apparently he'd lost track of time. Victor came to an area where he found what looked to be the bones of dead deer piled up in a small ditch on the sand. Victor's theory of dead wildlife around the lake looked like it might have been true after all.

Willy's description of the lake being three or four miles long imprinted on Victor's mind as he realized how far from home he might be. Whatever was on the other side of the lake that he wanted to take pictures of for his photography class probably wasn't something he should risk his life for.

When he finally reached the end of the lake there was nothing special to see that day, prompting Victor to decide to walk back into the woods again and make his way back home. The sun was beginning to set and it was time for him to eat dinner. Suddenly, as he turned, something caught his attention. There was something past the trees, which appeared to be some kind of house.

Victor went in to get a closer look, but passing the trees gave him an uneasy feeling. He found that the area around it stunk as he got closer. When he was walking near, he looked up at the house, which was as large as a mansion. He wondered who the house belonged to and began to investigate further. The house appeared really old, like it was from a different era. As he came close to the house he realized the front door was open. He walked up the stairs, pushed the door open and leaned inside, yelling out, "Hello!"

No one answered in the dark, mysterious house-like mansion. Victor would not put his foot through the front door without an invitation so he walked back down the stairs. Before he could leave, he stepped on something. It made a crunch-like sound and was partially buried. He reached down to pull it out; it appeared to be a blood-dried skull. The left eye of it was crumpled from Victor stepping on it, although it was clearly human. Victor quickly decided he had done enough sight-seeing and decided to run. He continued running down the shore with only one thought on his mind – to get back to his house safely.

As he was running, he tripped over a rock and fell, twisting his right ankle and landing on his side. He spotted another house off to the side beyond the trees. He lifted himself back up and walked towards it, crouching and peeking through one of the windows. Victor saw nothing, then suddenly Willy popped up and surprised him. Victor fell backward on the ground and Willy came outside asking, "Victor, what are you doing here?"

Victor got back up and said, "I was just walking down there. You lied to us about being the only ones here."

Now came the time for Willy to tell Victor the truth. Willy looked at Victor, feeling nervous for him. "You shouldn't have gone down there. I told you it would be dangerous."

"Willy, please tell me what is going on. Who killed those missing people? And who lives in that house?"

Willy hesitated to answer, thinking Victor wouldn't believe him, but he knew now that Victor's life was in danger and he had to know. "Alright, you really want to know?"

"Yes, please tell me!"

"Okay, nobody knows the legend better than me. What lives in that house are the Mallard Brothers."

Victor responded, "How many are there?"

"Four, and they've lived there for a long time."

"Do they have anything to do with the killings? Because I found a human skull in front of their house. And what do you mean; how long?"

Willy hesitated to answer again but muttered, "For over a hundred and eighty years."

Victor looked very puzzled and said, "That's impossible!"

"They're werewolves, Victor!"

"There's no such thing as a werewolf."

Yes there is. You'll hear them howl every night from your house."

"But tell me how it's possible. Where did they come from?"

"Well, it all started in the eighteen hundreds when the Mallard's came to this town. Their father owned this lake, and got men to build them an estate. For eighteen years they lived here, creating a paradise in the woods until one day someone, someone who had been searching for Jed Mallard for a long time..." And in Willy's words was the story of how the werewolves came to be.

"The reason the Mallard family came to America in the first place was to be free from the witch who tormented Jed for over half of his life. He had been her slave when he was a child, and had suffered under her cruel rule. Her worst acts happened when Jed was four years old. The evil witch saw fit to kill his parents in front of him. She treated him like she was his mother at times, though still cruel."

"In 1798, at the age of eighteen, he ran from her, never looking back, which started a hunt that carried on for years. For a year he was on the run from the witch, moving from place to place all over England. Jed knew that she could use her magic to help hunt him, but even with this to her advantage it had not been easy to follow his trail. When he turned nineteen, he lived in a small village and stayed there until he began to fear the witch would find him."

"So, in the year 1800, Jed made his way to London where he became a merchant and started trading with the French. For three months he was loyal to his job, until he became an accountant. During the next three years, he met a woman named Elizabeth, and Jed fell madly in love with her. He later married her and went on to have two boys."

"In the years he lived in London, Jed and his family became part of the fabric of society. One of Jed's best friends was one of the "town watchmen" who knew everybody in the city because his job required it. Jed asked him if he knew a woman named Mary Galloway that had come into the city."

"He described her as having blonde hair, young in appearance, beautiful, but with a witch-like quality about her. He asked his friend to warn him if he ever came across someone fitting this description, hoping that between him and his friend he would always be one step ahead of his enemy."

"In the year 1804, the witch made her way to London and instantly caught the eye of Jed's friend. He spoke to her, asking who she was, where she came from, and why she was here. She told him that she was from somewhere up north, and that she was here looking for the man she loved. He asked what his name was and she told him it was Jed Mallard. He immediately ran to Jed to warn him before she could find him in the city. Once Jed had been warned, he took his family to the docks and got on a ship that was heading toward America. Jed had warned his wife that this day would come."

"They sailed out onto the Atlantic, taking two months to sail to America where they were ready to make a new living. Jed could have planned an attack on her in London, but he was not going to risk his life now that he had a family counting on him. His plans that day were entirely defensive, hoping that the witch would not find him."

"When they arrived in Washington, D.C., Jed had the opportunity to speak with a man named Thomas Jefferson, who later became President. They had spoken of the plight of Jed and his family, as well as the opportunities that were opening up in America. Mr. Jefferson thought that since Jed was running away from something and was interested in disappearing, he might be convinced to travel inland by venturing with two local explorer-types named Lewis and Clark. These men had been given an order to venture to the northwest and make it to the Pacific Ocean by an overland route. Few joined their crew, only men with enough courage to journey on such an endeavor. Jefferson gave Jed a signed contract to show to Lewis and Clark, so they travelled west to St. Louis to meet up with them. They only had fourteen days to get there before the two explorers would begin their expedition."

"On the sixth day of their journey to St. Louis, they came to the town of Knoxville, Tennessee where they stayed the night in a hotel. The streets appeared rough, so Jed would not allow his family to go anywhere at night, nor would he let them leave his side during the day. After the boys went to sleep, Jed and his wife had a romantic night. Jed told his wife that being with her made him feel like he started his life all over again. He explained that he never had the best childhood and that being with her made the emptiness as a child, feel full again."

"The next morning Jed and his family woke up to leave and continued on their route to St. Louis, then came across a campsite where they spent the night to rest. They had seven days left to get to St. Louis. Until morning they huddled around a campfire to stay safe from the animals."

"Unknown to the family, someone was stalking them. Someone who had caught a horse and followed them to Tennessee."

"Over the next six days they continued their travels, finally arriving in St. Louis a day before Lewis and Clark were set to leave. Jed told them about his meeting with Thomas Jefferson and that they were sent to join them on their expedition. The pair were not comfortable at first bringing a man along with his family, but since Jefferson sent them then they had to accept it, hoping that the family wouldn't slow them down. The crew and passengers boarded the boats and began to sail up the Missouri River the next day. Moving against the swift river current took days and days, as they worried about the unknown. Fresh food and water was scarce and they had to stop to fish and hunt as they went along. It quickly became obvious to them that their journey would be long and hard. The seasons passed and before long the expedition was forced to stop and plan for the winter. They built a settlement camp with wooden walls around it for protection and small, simple shelters within. They called it Fort Mandan. As winter fell upon their fort away from home, they took shelter and settled in for the long winter ahead. Many weeks passed before they were able to get back on their journey."

"Along the way they met different Native Americans and began to trade with them as a means of diplomacy. This is when Lewis and Clark first met the beautiful native princess, Sacagawea. As fate would have it, she would soon learn to trust the visitors and joined them in their journey."

"After winter passed, it was now April 29, 1805, they left their fort and began to sail onward to the Yellowstone River in Montana. This was a huge open space where they encountered many new challenges and obstacles. One of the most ferocious ones was a massive grizzly bear, which Lewis and Clark ended up killing."

"In May, Lewis and Clark continued on their journey with their companions, sailing alongside them down the Yellowstone River. They arrived at a lake nestled between the mountains in an untouched valley, which Jed thought was beautiful. They knew from the start that this was home, and Jed decided he and his family would stay."

"Lewis and Clark asked if they were sure they wanted to stay and not come along to create history. Jed said that he didn't want to go, and that he would make history on his own here. They parted ways on good terms, while Lewis and Clark continued on their way to the Pacific, and Jed's family made their home on the lake. Lewis and Clark left them food and half a dozen men to help him build a settlement. Soon it would be a place for trade and travel for people to settle on arrival in Montana. For the next few months, Jed and his men finished building the settlement outside, near the lake. Each month it got bigger, chopping down more and more trees. They were trying to expand the area for more buildings, preparing for it to one day become a town. It later became a historic landmark."

"The next year, in 1806, Lewis and Clark discovered the northwest and reached the Pacific. After building a fort they named Fort Clatsop and living there for a few months, they made their way back to where they had ventured from. Although Lewis and Clark were heading back home, they divided their possessions and each made new routes back. Lewis travelled through northern Montana and Clark travelled through the southern part of Montana. Once Lewis came to Jed's settlement, he couldn't believe how much they had expanded and improved it. He told Jed that he and Clark had reached the Pacific and that they were heading back to St. Louis to spread the word."

"One day when Jed and the others were working out in the fields, his wife Elizabeth was alone in the house, and a man attacked her. Jed wouldn't have known if he hadn't left her a dueling pistol to fire off if anything happened. The oldest son had tried to stop the attack, but was slapped with a backhand across the face and fell to the ground. The man's language was frightening to her."

"The attacker told her he was interested in her since the day he first saw her, when they were leaving Knoxville. Jed, upon hearing the gunshot, started to run to her rescue as the man ripped her clothes off. Fortunately, Jed got there in time. Jed pulled him off the table he had thrown his wife onto, slamming him against the floor. The man got back up quickly and started to go for the gun Jed had given to Elizabeth earlier. Jed tried to attack the man, but when he saw him reaching for the gun, Elizabeth found a knife on the ground and, just in time, plunged it through his arm before Jed could do anything else. She plunged the knife in so hard that it stuck in the ground, along with the man's arm. He tried to pull it out with his left hand, but Elizabeth got to the gun first and, looking at him with hysteria, she shot him dead. Jed and Elizabeth looked at each other in disbelief, then she rushed into his arms as they clung to each other."

"Lewis informed Jed that he wouldn't have let this happen if he had known what kind of man he was, but despite what happened, he was glad to see that Jed and his wife had their third child, another son. After Lewis' visit, it was time to meet up with Clark along the way back to St. Louis."

"In 1809, as more people came there to live, they planned to have an election between Jed and a Liberal Democrat from Washington, D.C. The man wanted to be Mayor since they hadn't proclaimed one yet, even though Jed had started it all. Jed was upset when he found out Jefferson had sent the man to take over. Since Thomas Jefferson was no longer the president, Jed told him they didn't need him because he was their leader. But since he was ordered to be there and nobody was appointed mayor yet, there would have to be an election. For five days the election went on, and when all the votes were in, they began to count how many each had. The Democrat had thirty-nine votes and Jed had ninety-eight."

"After Jed won the election, the Democrat became fed up and left the town, swearing he would take over as mayor one day. The town celebrated his election and Jed decided to give their new home a name, calling it 'Roarke'. The town was happy as it would stand for all time."

"As the years went by, Roarke was doing better than ever. The population was growing, the town was expanding, and life was better than it had ever been. It had now been five years since Jed won the election. Back in 1810, a year after the election, Jed and his wife had their fourth child, and this too was a baby boy."

"In 1814, on his 32nd birthday, Jed told his wife that he was going to travel to Virginia to see if he could find any workers and perhaps convince more people to help colonize the town. His wife did not feel comfortable with the idea of him leaving them, but he convinced her that he would be back soon."

"The path back to St. Louis took less time by following Lewis and Clark's trail. He travelled for nearly three months until he came to the state of

Missouri. He did not find Lewis and Clark, though he did see some people who recognized him after seeing him leave from their great journey ten years previous. He stayed the night in St. Louis, and the next day he made his way to Virginia. For the next eight days, he rounded up people willing to work to keep his town alive and vibrant. Each man that worked would get an equal share. Jed also bought cattle to herd back to Roarke with his crew. Because of all of this, it took nearly five months to head back home."

"When Jed finally made it back, his wife was happy to see him and he was happy to see her too. All four of his sons seemed to have grown up to him, so much so that he wondered why time couldn't have gone by faster when he was young. Jed just hoped that he could leave behind what he had done while he was away, like nothing had ever happened. He did not like withholding important information from his wife such as the fact that his childhood was a nightmare and that his parents were killed, but it seemed to be worth it."

"The next year, in 1815, he took his oldest son, James, hunting. He was fourteen now and that would basically be a man to them. They hunted for quail since they seemed overpopulated in that area. When Jed scared a few out of the trees by the river, Jed and James started shooting. They killed nine in the air, though Jed only killed three; his son killed double that."

"It was unbelievable. Jed knew that God had given his son the gift of excellent marksmanship. Six kills, six perfect shots, no misses. For the rest of the year, Jed would take James hunting. Once they even killed a grizzly, as it looked like it would snap them in half. When James was close to turning fifteen, he was finished with school and decided to go off to work. He decided he'd either be farmer or a deputy in town, knowing that he was skilled with a gun. He tried both, at first as a farmer and part-time deputy, then he decided to just be a lawman. James' younger brothers, Albert, Ben and Nate, were all still in school. Albert was nearly finished since he was close to fourteen."

"June 12, 1816, a trader came to Roarke, putting the word out that he wanted to see Jed. Eventually one of the sheriff's deputies brought him to see Jed, and the sheriff followed to see what was going on. The trader walked up to see Jed in his office with the sheriff close behind him. Before the sheriff noticed, the trader had pulled a knife. When Jed saw him going for the knife, he grabbed his arm and threw the man to the floor. The man got back up and as he did, the sheriff came at the man with a punch. The man ducked and the punch missed. The sheriff turned around and as he did, a punch returned by the stranger landed square on the sheriff's chin, sending him to the ground. As the sheriff hit the ground and the man was about to come down on him with his knife, Jed pulled out a pistol from his drawer, pointing it at the man and shooting him in the ribs. The bullet hit, stopping the stranger in his tracks as he fell against the wall. The knife dropped to his side, within reach of the sheriff who kicked it out of the way, scrambling to cuff the man so there could be no more surprises. Everyone was in shock as the doctor came to treat the stranger before transporting him to the cell. His screams could be heard by everyone due to the pain from the doctor digging the bullet out of his rib cage."

"Who was this guy and why did he want to kill Jed? Lots of questions and no answers led to rumors running wild around town. Three hours later, Jed went to see the man and find out why he had tried to kill him. When he did, he found out that the man was actually a hired assassin. He told Jed that he was sent by a man named John Pelts, and that he'd had a grudge against Jed for years. He had gathered his own following and wanted to take what he thought should have been his. His first plan was to assassinate Jed and take over the town, becoming mayor himself. From what the stranger knew, if that failed, he planned to send in members of his little army to fight. If the assassin did not return within four hours, the assault would begin."

"After Jed and the sheriff received all the information they needed from the prisoner, they prepared themselves for what might follow. One of the first steps was to put oil in the fields so that when the enemy came they could surprise them by setting fire to the fields, hoping to bring down their numbers a bit. The next measure was to gather dynamite and set them in place for their second surprise. They also gathered guns for a long range assault on anyone that made it through the fields of fire and explosions."

"The people in the village were willing to follow Jed in this fight; some were simply loyal and others were too confused to understand what was going on as it had all happened so fast. An hour later, Jed and his men were waiting for John and his men to arrive. When they finally arrived, their appearance caught Jed off guard. Some of the men didn't look like soldiers, they looked more like bandits. It looked like he had hired a few people as mercenaries to help him take Roarke. As John and his men were coming out of the trees, there looked to be about three hundred and they looked strong. John sent in the first wave, and when they got into the fields of tall dry grass, Jed's men set off the oil traps by throwing torches into the grass while hiding behind trees off to the side. After that, Jed's men ran back through the settlement gate."

"Almost half of John's men were burning to death and couldn't run out of the field fast enough because the fire spread through the field in the blink of an eye. Once the fire cleared, John was furious and ordered his men to charge the settlement. When they were about a hundred feet away, Jed ordered his men to fire their guns at them from above the walls. Before John's men could even make it forty feet to the town's walls, the dynamite hidden under the hay that was attached to wires from the gate were lit, and men were exploding all around them. At this point there were probably only one hundred forty of their enemies left. John's men came with ladders and used them to climb over the walls. One of the defenders on the walls was Jed's son, James, who had joined the fight without Jed's knowledge."

"During the fight, Jed and his men must have killed ten more, but they lost some men in their group too. Some of John's men brought dynamite of their own to the gate. As soon as James saw that it was going to ignite, he warned the others to clear the area. He ran off the wall and when the gate blew up, so did some of Jed and John's men. Only a few could outrun the explosion. Once the gate was blown up, the rest of John's men charged in to try to take the town while Jed pulled his men back to the town square. When they got to the town square, Jed and his men realized they were running out of options. They took their guns, some of them crouching down and some standing behind them, ready to fire. They killed six more of John's men as they charged down the street.

They reloaded and fired again, killing six more."

"Jed had all the women and children safe in the town hall with the doors barricaded. When John's men got to them, Jed and his men fought as hard as they could, sending fear into the eyes of John's men. Once they got through Jed's human wall of men all over the settlement, it became a fair fight as the numbers were much closer now due to the advanced strikes Jed had devised. It just became a question of who would win."

"As the battle continued, John left his command to find Jed and kill him, knowing he would not get another chance like this. Jed tried to find his son, but he was nowhere to be seen. During the battle James hid, then fled to take refuge. James heard someone coming and got ready to shoot. When the person entered, he popped out from the sheriff's desk and held the gun toward the man. Fortunately, he was able to identify him before pulling the trigger. It was one of his fellow deputies. He told him that it was crazy out there, so he too decided to take refuge in the building and wait it out. After about five minutes they changed their minds and decided to go out and join the fight again. The deputy went out first and when he did, he was shot in the head by a sharpshooter rifle."

"The shooter was the prisoner who they had had

in custody; he had gotten out and was now hiding in the upstairs window of the town's mercantile. He looked through the scope to see if there was anyone else coming out of the office."

"James thought about taking the risk of running out, but didn't since he knew if the shooter was able to kill the deputy that fast, he would be waiting for him to exit the building. James knew that if he stayed too long, he would be trapped. He realized that one option was to kick through the boards in the jailhouse, hoping to break a hole in them to escape through the other side, out of the shooter's sight. When he finished kicking out the boards, he snuck around the jailhouse to the end of the street. James wanted to make a run to the other side of the street and get behind the mercantile, giving the assassin a surprise attack."

"There were five other of John's men running down the street. The assassin yelled out to them from the window that he was with them and that there was someone else inside the jailhouse. They went inside to find James, only to see that he had escaped. The assassin ordered them to search for him as James quietly made his way inside the building to kill him. The assassin had kept it dark inside, knowing he would be nearly invisible until anyone entering's eyes adjusted."

"James made his way up the stairs, hoping the floorboards wouldn't creak, wondering which of the rooms the shooter could be in. When he finally made his way slowly upstairs and was about to open the first door, he heard a gunshot coming from the room down the hall. He quickly yet quietly stepped down the hall until suddenly, as he put all of his weight on a weak board, it made a loud creak. The assassin heard the squeaky board and returned his eye to the scope with a grin on his face."

"The men searching for James shouted to the assassin that they couldn't find him, and he again ordered them to keep searching, that he was around here somewhere. James came to the assassin's room with his back against the wall, his left hand on the door, and the rifle in his right. He peeked through the door, took a few seconds to get ready to hold his breath, then slammed the door open with his left arm, putting both arms on the rifle in marking position. The assassin wasn't at the window, but his rifle was left sitting there. James quickly pointed his gun all around the room but the assassin was nowhere to be seen."

"Out of nowhere the assassin appeared with a Tranter revolver. Spotting him from the corner of his eye, he quickly used his rifle to deflect the assassin's gun by pushing it up, above both their heads. As they had their arms up, the assassin used his right leg to kick James back. James landed on the ground and immediately tried to shoot the assassin with his rifle, but the assassin was long gone, outside the room, while two gunshots were fired. The shots alerted the men outside, and they dashed inside to find out who was shooting. The assassin made his way downstairs and got his followers to go up after James. James grabbed the sharpshooter rifle and went outside the window. He shimmied across the ledge and climbed up to the roof, with his shadow covering the light from the window of the second floor room he had crawled out of."

"One of the men that ran into the room saw the shadow, realizing it was someone right outside the window. He walked over to the window as the shadow passed, letting the sunlight through, and then he opened it, looking up. He followed him, lifting himself up onto the roof. He took up his gun, though there was no sign of James. The man looked to his left and saw a man with a sharpshooter on the roof of the building next door to the mercantile… it was James. As soon as the man saw him, James shot a bullet through his chest, causing him to fall off the roof, alerting the other men."

"A few men ran out to find the dead body, realizing James must have jumped onto the other roof since the buildings were so close. James then shot one of these men in the neck. They started to run back inside, but before they could, one was shot in the back, killing him. The man spurting blood from his neck begged for help, and one of the others gave him a thick piece of fabric to wrap tightly across the wound, trying to stop the bleeding."

"To avoid being stuck and surrounded by the remaining men, James climbed down off the roof by sliding down the pole."

"In anger, the assassin furiously forced them to get back out there and kill James, convincing them that he was just a boy and that they had nothing to fear. The two men ran outside, rapidly firing at the rooftop James was on, while the third was still inside bleeding. As the assassin watched the two of them outside, the injured man, still holding his hand against the wound, took his other hand and reached it out to the assassin, begging for help. The assassin exited the building, leaving him behind as the man fell down, slowly dying due to blood loss. The other two men, who were outside, stopped shooting and reloaded their guns."

"James, who had now snuck back to the other side of the street, could hear the shells being emptied and knew it was the perfect time for him to strike back. Both their backs were facing James, thinking he might still be on the roof or somewhere inside the building."

"The two oblivious men started to take up their

guns again, but not before James ran down the alley to shoot them both in the back with his revolver. All that was left now was the assassin. James hid. Despite how well he was doing, he feared his enemy. He made his way back to the jailhouse and took cover behind the wall. He could hear a horse galloping past the jailhouse, so he carefully peeked out, crouching down with his head looking around past the door. It was the assassin, running away on horseback. The further away he got, the harder the shot was, so James took out the repeater rifle, pointing it at him with an impossible range of fire. He was out of bullets for the sharp shooter so he had to shoot without the gun and its incredible precision. James went ahead and took the shot. As the bullet flew, it hit the assassin's back, puncturing his right lung. He fell off the horse, landing on his back. He got back up, winded. "

"James ran up to him, looking down at him with disdain. He thought about him killing his fellow deputy, and trying to kill his father. The assassin looked up at him with a weary yet rather impressed look. Then, of course, James put him down with his revolver, not realizing that his father was watching."

"As James turned around, he caught his father's eye, seeing how uneasy he looked. Jed told him that he was glad he was safe and that it was time they put an end to this once and for all."

"While some of the others were still fighting in the town square, Jed led the others, wanting to flank the enemy. He could see John on a horse, riding down the street that led to the town square. When the time was right, Jed got his men together, planning to surprise John and the men he was with. Once they passed, the men charged from inside the buildings and killed all the men except John. At that point, Jed sent his men off to fight the rest of John's men in the town square. John's men were feeling defeated seeing that they were now surrounded and leaderless. They began to retreat, but Jed wouldn't allow it, worried that if even just one lived they would return to fight again."

"After a long day of fighting, Jed and the rest of the townspeople struggled to heal from their mourning over the dead, but soon disposed of John and his men's bodies. Many town residents wished they had killed him themselves, but with the battle over, within a few days they had put away their anger. Word had reached even the President of Jed's exploit and how he defended his town. A letter was sent to Jed, telling him how impressed the President was and that he was being awarded a Medal of Valor for his bravery."

"Time passed, and the year was now 1830. Jed and his family were growing tremendously well. James had joined the army, ranked Captain, and was the best shot in his regiment. Albert, the next oldest, went to university to become a doctor. Ben was the more adventurous one, dreaming of one day being like Lewis and Clark and travelling north. Nate started to work at the mercantile that James had his gun fight in, although he sometimes joined Ben on his journeys."

"It seemed like everything was perfect. Three years after the attack, Jed had a house built, an estate. It had room to spare and every summer the boys would come to stay with them on the lake, but unfortunately the summer of 1830 would be their last."

"Something was near, Jed could feel its presence. His feeling of fear had faded, just as the memory of his old enemy, the witch, had faded. That is until he saw a cloaked figure walking on the sands toward his home. He knew it would have to be her, as that same fear came back just as it was the last time he saw her. Jed ran back to his home to prepare himself. He made a quick note of his thoughts in his journal, knowing they might be his last. He then took his gun and tried to sneak up behind her. When she approached the house, she turned and saw Jed as if she had already known he was there. Before he could get a shot off, she cast a spell. He fell to the ground, feeling numb in his stomach. The gun hit the ground, triggering a shot."

"After hearing the shot, Elizabeth came out, knife

in hand, to see what was happening. She saw the face she had dreaded seeing, and instinctively charged at the witch. The witch cast another spell on Elizabeth, and this one was more deadly than the one she had cast on Jed. Elizabeth fell to the ground, dead. Just moments after, their sons ran out and saw what had happened. The witch was surprised to see that Jed had a family, and insisted to Jed that she could be their new mother, with her as his new bride. Jed refused. Since she could not have his love, she decided she would destroy them. But instead of killing his sons, she cursed them to become werewolves."

"Jed thought back to the time in England when he had his chance to kill her and be done with this curse forever. He was not going to allow his sons to have this fate. As he struggled to get up with his gun, he slowly stood up in pain, shooting and killing the witch from behind with a single shot in the back. But he was too late to save his sons from being turned into monsters. Jed then fell back, dead from the spell the witch had cast upon him."

"From that point on, people started disappearing at the lake, and exactly what happened to the Mallard family remains a mystery to this day," said Willy.

"It sure sounds like an urban legend, Willy, but I have to ask. How do you know all of this?"

"Well, it's because my great, great grandfather was the caretaker of that house. When the witch approached their house, the caretaker, following Jed's order, ran away with the journal Jed had used to record his life over all those years."

Willy pulled the journal from the drawer, showing it to Victor and said, "It's been passed down from father to son. Now I suggest you get your family out of that house because I don't want you to get killed like the couple that lived in your house before. This is especially true since you've just walked onto their territory, and they hunt down anyone that goes near their house."

"Do they turn human when it's daylight?"

Willy replied, "No, the witch cursed them to forever, even in daytime, to be werewolves. They don't see as well in the daytime, so they stay in the basement where it's dark until night comes."

Realizing he had been gone for a long time, Victor ran saying, "I've got to get back."

As Victor ran back to warn his parents, he knew it wasn't going to be easy. The sun looked like it was going down and it was getting darker. Victor ran inside the house and his mother asked where he'd been. Victor didn't answer, but instead asked, "Mom, where's Dad and Natalie?"

"Your father is at the shop, and Natalie took the other car into town."

"Mom, we have to leave or they're going to kill us!"

"What are you talking about, who's going to kill us?"

"You wouldn't believe me if I told you. Just trust me on this, we need to leave."

"We're not going anywhere!"

Victor began to shout, trying to convince his mom. "I don't care how, we'll walk out of here. Now let's go!"

"No, if this is about that hermit, well I don't want you going near him anymore."

Victor knew what needed to be done, so he grabbed an ornament off the shelf to knock her out. He hit her from behind, on the top of the head. She fell to the ground, but Victor managed to get her up and out of the house. He carried her out onto the road by placing her over his shoulder and onto his back. She was lighter than him, so he could manage carrying her far enough into town. Victor wanted to get to the shop fast, so he could find a phone to call Natalie before she went back to the house. This was one of Victor's scariest moments. It became a race and he hated races, but this was his to win.

Chapter Four

As Victor was moving toward his father's shop carrying his mother, Willy made his way to the Mallard house. He set dynamite all around the house. He was planning to blow the house on top of the werewolves, not knowing the werewolves were already out. As he grabbed his whisky bottle and took a drink, he heard a growl coming from behind him. He slowly turned around and there he saw it – a werewolf. He could hear them all around the clearing as he stood in front of the house. When they charged at him, he shouted, "No!"

After they were finished with Willy, they picked up Victor's scent and began to go on the hunt for him.

When Victor finally got to town with his mom, he saw Natalie drive by in one of their cars. Natalie stopped and asked, "What happened to Mom?"

Victor lied, "She had an accident. Take us to see Dad."

Victor got into the car with his mom and Natalie, as Natalie started driving to the shop. It was around

9:00 p.m. and David's shop was already closed with the shutters down. When he saw them pull up, he was standing outside the shop. He bent down, hands on the window sill, looking inside the car. When he saw Susan he asked, "What happened?"

Victor was still acting as though it was an accident. Victor was not the greatest at making decisions, but he had to try since the fate of his family depended on it. He then heard a loud howl coming all the way from the lake. He demanded that his dad open the shop.

"No, why? I mean, it's closed now."

"Dad, we have to get in, they're coming!"

"What are you talking about? Who's coming?"

Victor got out of the car with his mom, and started to carry her unconscious body into Ollie's, right as they were closing. David and Natalie chased after him as he went inside. "Oh, right on time. I was just about to close!" said Ollie.

Victor spoke up and said, "Mr. Ollie, I need you to close the shutters on the windows quickly!"

"I will, but I need you all to leave the store first."

"We can't. There are people out there trying to kill us!"

Ollie knew to trust Victor from the solemn look on his face. He quickly followed Victor's instructions, and began closing the shutters, planning to call the cops when he was done. He closed the shutters on both the windows, and was getting ready to close the ones at the door when someone appeared late to buy something. It was Steven. Victor ran to the door to speak to him and when he got there, he saw someone running behind him. Victor quickly opened the door and dragged Steven in, while Ollie closed the shutters.

"What's wrong with you, Victor?"

At that moment, before Victor could answer, the werewolves slammed on the shutters from outside the doors. As they listened to the growling outside, Steven asked, "What is that, a bear?"

"No, it's a werewolf," replied Victor.

Everyone looked at Victor as Natalie asked, "What do you mean… a werewolf?"

"Exactly what I just said! Listen, Willy told me everything and not only was I told, but I've basically seen it."

David walked up and Victor again said, "Dad, I'm sorry, I tried to tell you."

"Look Victor, let's just say I don't believe you, but I'll protect you and buy the part that you say we're in danger."

Steven was hiding with a baseball bat he had found in a drawer under the clerk's till. David asked, "Did you try calling the cops yet?"

Ollie said, "No, not yet!" and went behind the counter. Steven was sitting down with the bat as he tried using the phone, not realizing the old phone was gone and they had to install a new one. He asked his clerk, "Where is the phone?"

The clerk, Reggie answered, "I'm sorry, but it crashed just last night when I was working with Delmar."

David said, "Well then, I guess we'll just wait it out till dawn when someone will come."

Steven stood up from behind the till and shouted, "I can't stay here, I've got to get home!"

Victor was trying to convince Steven, "You can't go! You have to stay here or they'll kill you. By tomorrow they'll be gone."

"And how do you know they won't get in here?"

"I don't, I just know we'll be safer in here until then, and we definitely won't be safe if we try to leave."

Steven sat back down, and David took his wife and daughter to the back office to remain safe. He had Natalie watch over her mom until she woke up. They heard a noise on the roof, which they thought might be one of the werewolves, but soon it became quiet again. An hour went by and still nothing.

It was around 10:00 p.m. and there was no sound from the wolves. Victor went behind the till to speak with Steven and sat down with him. He asked Steven, "How are you?"

Steven looked up and said, "I'm fine, I guess. So, are these werewolves the cause for all the disappearances?"

"Yes, and they're here because I walked onto their territory."

"Who are they and where do they come from?"

"Well they ain't from Cleveland!"

"Seriously, you're going to pull out jokes now?!"

"Sorry, it's just I think it's okay to laugh when you already know you're going to be okay."

"So what happens in the morning? Are we really going to be safe until then?"

"They can't stand the sun, so they'll retreat back to the lake. Willy told me that there was a family called the Mallard's who had been hiding from a witch all the way from England. The witch found them, killed the parents and cursed the sons to be werewolves. The witch was also killed by the father in the process, just before he died. Ever since then, people have gone missing. The father, Jed, was the mayor – the founder of this town when it was first built. So you see Steven, werewolves exist, as do witches and god knows what else."

After hearing that, Steven asked, "So, what are we going to do if we have to fight back?"

"I don't know but is it like what you see in movies, that werewolves die from silver?"

"Well yes, it is their strongest weakness, but I read about a man from another time who killed a werewolf with a shovel. What I'm saying to you, Victor, is that I think you can kill one with anything you have."

"So maybe if we took a shotgun and shot off one

of their heads, would it work?" Victor questioned.

"Yes, I mean even though superhuman, they should be able to die from anything just like people, like that witch you spoke of getting killed from anything."

"I didn't say anything, but she did get shot in the back."

"Exactly! So I think my theory is correct," Steven said excitedly.

Steven felt better, but was still nervous at the thought of having to fight the wolves. "So where's Willy the Hillbilly?"

Victor was getting mad, "Don't call him that!"

"Well what's wrong? It's just a name."

"He may be a hermit, but he's a good man. He warned me to keep me safe."

Victor was about to get up and leave but Steven stopped him, "Victor wait, I'm sorry. I know that was rude and it's definitely not necessary at a time like this. I even hear he was once friends with Ollie."

"Really?" asked Victor.

"Yeah, apparently they had a greaser gang back in the fifties. Willy was the leader until sometime during the war. I don't know too much about his life after his greaser days, but I believe his dad owned the barber shop your dad owns now."

"How could I not know this?"

"He really didn't tell you?"

"No, I don't think he really knew. I mentioned it once to him, but didn't say it was the Snider Barber Shop. So I suppose his last name is Snider?"

"Yes, it is!" said Ollie after overhearing their conversation. "Willy and I were friends back in the day. I was still in high school and he was in his twenties."

"Is it true you were in a gang?" asked Steven.

"It wasn't like a gang, I mean we may have done some things that were illegal but we were good people. Well, at least most of us."

"What do you mean?" asked Victor.

"Well, Willy was the one who called the shots. He was our leader and I guess some of the things he did we were in together. Wanting to stay out of more trouble, some of us followed and would help cover his mistakes. I myself didn't want to have anything to do with it, so I left."

"What did Willy do?" asked Victor.

Ollie gave them both a look of distress, but before he could answer, Victor's mom regained consciousness. David walked up to her and asked, "Are you okay?"

"I'm fine. Victor hit me on the head!" answered Susan with her hand on top of her head. Susan wondered why they were there and why everyone looked like they were waiting for something. She asked, "What's going on? Where are we?"

Everyone began talking at the same time, "We were chased in here by werewolves! Victor was carrying you into town, I was coming in here to buy something, then I was pulled in by Victor. Things started smashing on the shutters from outside, there's no phone, and we can't leave till dawn," everyone quickly told her.

Susan was overwhelmed with the incredible news and said, "Hey, one at a time! I am beginning to get a headache from all this talking after getting hit on the head."

She then walked up to Victor and said, "Victor, I'm sorry I didn't believe you."

"It's alright, Mom."

"But was it really necessary to hit me on the head?

"Yes, because you weren't listening to me and I couldn't just leave you to die."

Susan asked wearily, "Where are they now?"

"We don't know. We haven't heard a sound from them for a while, but the good news is they will be gone by daylight."

There weren't many people out at this time of night in a small town like this, but suddenly they heard a crash coming from outside. They couldn't see what was happening since all the shutters were closed, but Ollie went to grab the key and opened the door just enough to peek outside to see what was happening.

They saw a car that had crashed into a telephone pole outside on the street, but no one else was in sight. The man was getting out of his car, looking around like he'd seen something run in front of his car before crashing. He took a good look around him, then noticed Ollie peeking from behind the window.

He waved and yelled, "Hey, could you help me? I believe my car's totaled and I think I may have hit some animal, but I don't know!"

Ollie looked back at everyone as they were wondering if they should let him in or not. Victor was scared of what might happen if they did. The man again yelled, "Hey, do you hear me? My car is wrecked, and I need you to call someone to come pick it up!"

They felt obligated to go out and help, so David and Ollie volunteered. Before they could open the shutters to go out, they heard the man yell, then scream, "Help!" before banging on the door. "Someone please open the door! There's something out here!"

Ollie quickly opened the shutter door less than half way so the man could crawl in, allowing them to close it fast enough to keep anything else out. He broke much of the glass and shutters at the bottom of the door so the man could crawl through the door, hoping he would not cut himself while crawling through the hole. The man began crawling through but before he could get in, he was pulled out and mauled by one of the werewolves.

David dropped to the ground to see what was happening. After seeing the man being attacked, another werewolf appeared, scratching David on the face, surprising him by sticking his arm in at the bottom of the shutters. David pulled himself away from the door and yelled, "Close it!"

Ollie turned the key and the shutters began closing on the werewolf's arm. The werewolf started to pull his arm out, but it looked like his arm was going to be stuck. Unfortunately the werewolf was strong enough to pull it out, leaving a small dent at the bottom of the shutters.

Reggie stepped up and said, "What's wrong with you, old man?!"

"What are you saying, Reggie?" asked Ollie.

"You could have just opened up the shutters more, then the man would've gotten in before they snagged him."

"I wanted to, but I couldn't."

"Yeah sure – you couldn't. That man is dead now because of you!"

"Will you keep your voice down, you fucking prick!" said Victor.

"Yeah, no disrespect kid, but no one is talking to

you. And you know what! I take that back, it's not his fault. It's your fault! You brought them here, and now a man is dead because of you."

"If Ollie had opened up the shutters all the way, those things would still have gotten to him, not to mention they would have probably broken through the glass doors and tried to kill all of us."

"Whatever! Just know that it's still your fault."

After that, Reggie walked away from both Ollie and Victor as he sneakily crept to the back to have a cigarette.

Once again the wolves remained quiet, as if they just left and weren't coming back. But Victor knew that probably wasn't the case and that they would stop at nothing. The time was now 4:27 a.m., getting close to daylight.

It had been three hours since the attack. Even though the time came close for the werewolves to leave, people were growing rather impatient, especially Reggie. He stayed in the back the entire time, and hadn't come out since the incident happened. Steven went to the back to check on him. Steven stood next to him as Reggie said, "You want a smoke?"

"No thanks, not my thing."

"Might as well since this could be your last night."

Steven took him up on his offer and tried it, resulting in a few coughs.

They seemed to have grown some kind of trust in one another as Reggie tried to befriend Steven. He went on saying, "You know, someone's got to do something, unlike those pussies in the other room. I can't believe I even work for that guy now – and that kid, your buddy. What's his name?"

"Victor."

"Yeah, Victor. I mean, it's his fault we're even in this mess. You just came here to buy something and that… asshole dragged you into it."

"Yes, but he also says by sometime today they will go away."

"Yeah, and how exactly do you think we can hold out till that time? Look at me. They're not after us. They're after him. If we hand him over to them, they'll let us go."

"But that's… that's like murder, man."

"Yeah well, it's worth it. You see that door? If you could lure him back here, we could knock him unconscious and bring him out through the back."

"I didn't know there was a back door; couldn't they have broken through that earlier?"

"No, it's steel, it's very strong. But anyway, we can do this. Just get him to come back here and we'll throw him out through the back."

Steven stood up and said, "No, forget it, I'm not doing it."

Steven walked out of the backroom to go see Victor and tell him about Reggie, but before he could, the wolves started banging on the shutters from outside. They still couldn't get through; however, one saw the dent that was now at the bottom, and used his hand to lift the shutter doors open. Ollie immediately took the key to try to bring it back down. As he turned the key, the shutters started closing, making the werewolf struggle. The rest of the pack joined to help lift, as they could all now put their hands under it to lift it up. The strength of the entire pack made it easier for them to pull it up, despite Ollie trying to shut them down.

Everyone retreated to the back room with Ollie leading them to the other door. Victor was the last to make it to the back door, and when he did, Reggie jumped at him and tried to get a hold of him. Victor quickly knocked him off by using his elbow, hitting Reggie on the right side of his head, causing him to fall back behind him. Victor ran up to the door but then stopped to look back at Reggie. By that time the werewolves had gotten through the front door shutters and began charging toward them. Reggie got up and tried to make a run for it to the door, but one of the werewolves caught up to him. One pinned him to the ground while another started running toward Victor. Victor stepped out and quickly swung the door shut. He could hear Reggie screaming from inside as the werewolves started carving him up with their claws, killing him.

Victor was alone. He tried to find his family, but needed a place to hide. He bumped into Steven and asked, "Steven, where is my family?"

"I don't know, we got separated. Where's Reggie?"

"He's dead, let's go."

As they heard one of the werewolves howl, they knew they needed to get out of the middle of the street. Steven still had the bat with him, but Victor needed a weapon. They soon came upon the hardware store, and the first thing that came to Victor's mind was a chainsaw. Victor looked down to his right as he quickly emptied a garbage can and threw it through the window glass. Victor knew the werewolves had probably heard all the noise, but they got inside and Victor was able to find a chainsaw. Victor and Steven made their way down the street to find Ollie and Victor's family.

Steven stuttered, "Victor, I tried to tell you, but Reggie had a plan to kill you. He thought if we handed you over, the wolves would leave us alone, but I walked away."

"He attacked me back at the store. I got him off and then the wolves attacked him."

"He really was an asshole."

"Yeah, but I wasn't going to leave him. I waited at the door, but it was too late; they already got to him. Let's just find my family and get out of here. It's got to be around 5:00 a.m."

Victor and Steven soon came across a narrow alley. Victor took the lead but then stopped when he saw a shadow appear. It got smaller, meaning the person was getting closer, but it did not sound human. Victor gave Steven a hand signal to go back. They quietly made their way back down the alley and hid behind the walls. The wolf appeared, making his way down the alley, scratching his claws on the walls.

Victor looked at Steven. He tried hinting to him that they should make a surprise attack. Victor pointed at the baseball bat he was carrying and then pointed at his knee joint, meaning he wanted Steven to jab the wolf in the leg as he came by. Steven gave him a nervous nod and held the bat up high, getting ready to swing it. Step by step the wolf got closer and closer. Steven swung the bat from high to low, hard, but there was nothing there. They looked at the wall with claw marks and then the other which looked like marks from a wolf climbing up. They followed the trail of claw marks right up the wall and saw the wolf looking down at them, taunting them. He leaped off the roof and landed on top of Steven. Steven had the bat in both his hands and used it keep the wolf from biting him. Victor ran over, starting the chainsaw. The wolf was choking on the bat, still trying to bite Steven. Steven looked at Victor and pointed his right arm out to perhaps hit or scratch him, but Victor swung the chainsaw and cut the werewolf's arm clean off. The werewolf jumped off of Steven and retreated to recover from his pain. Victor helped Steven up, while Steven thanked him.

They heard the loud howling of the suffering werewolf who was in great pain, rapidly losing blood, and it could not stand the agony of losing its arm. They then heard the howls of its brothers feeling the same agony, which lasted until it was time for them to leave. One of the werewolves, however, stayed and sniffed out Victor and Steven's presence, running from two legs to four at a reckless pace.

Victor and Steven finally found Ollie, along with Victor's family, who were hiding in the pharmacy store. Victor ran in to give his family a hug and then headed out again. Victor peeked outside the door, checking out his surroundings. The wolf looked directly at Victor from across the road. He charged at Victor, then leaped towards him. Victor immediately ducked as his dad stepped in front of him to protect him. David had an axe raised high in his hands and swung it down at the wolf, but the wolf dodged the blow by moving to the right, causing the axe to hit the ground. The wolf slammed against David as the axe hit the ground. Ollie made his move, using a knife he carried from his store. But again the werewolf dodged the attack, ducking then lifting Ollie above his head, throwing him into the wall. Susan and Natalie both stepped in, but the werewolf quickly pushed them away by placing his hands on their shoulders, pushing them to opposite sides and out of the way. He finally got to Victor, who was having trouble starting the chainsaw. Victor tried pushing him away with the chainsaw when he got close but the wolf disarmed him.

The wolf went in for a bite while Victor tried to use his elbow to keep him away, remaining in his stance. As Victor's arm got weaker, the wolf's mouth got closer. Victor released his elbow and the wolf slid past Victor, falling to the ground due to the effort of pushing forward toward Victor. The wolf got back up and tried to make another move, but the sun shone brightly, blinding the werewolf.

Victor went back to start the chainsaw and the wolf began to behave erratically, throwing his arms in the air. Victor tried getting in closer, moving his neck back to avoid being sliced by the werewolf's claws. With no mercy, Victor swung the chainsaw and chopped the werewolf's head off. His family just looked at him with concern.

Within an hour or two Victor and his dad had disposed of the wolves' bodies, which had turned back to human form after they died. They found the second one looked like he had bled to death from his wound. As for the bodies of Reggie and the stranger, they wondered how they were going to explain it to the police as an animal attack. They knew the police would probably realize there was more to what they were saying, but hopefully no one would think they were the killers. What would happen if the truth of the night's events was revealed?

Chapter Five

Letting bygones be bygones and through the darkness of life, there will be no regrets. The only way to find peace is to first forgive yourself and accept that they were your mistakes. Even friends can be deceivers and are capable of uprising. But to run away is to run from your guilt and to leave what you've left undone, and even more what you've left behind.

Willy's story began when he was a young man graduating from high school in 1947, sometime after the Second World War. In 1948, he was accepted into the University of Montana in Missoula. After being there for four months, he decided to study mechanics. While there, he tried to avoid making friends since he wasn't very good at that in high school. However, there was a young man who he met named Billy. He met Willy in class and the two hung out throughout most of the semester. Billy was from Lincoln, and came to university to study mechanics also. Willy joined the football team and was really good at it since he had played in high school. The girls thought Willy was handsome, and he soon became a big man on campus. Billy was still his friend, but was always considered 'the other guy' when he was with Willy, and soon grew to be extremely jealous of him. A girl who Billy had a crush on liked Willy, which set him off, making him decide to end their friendship. Willy tried to assure him that he wouldn't do anything to hurt Billy and hadn't since they'd first met, but Billy knew they couldn't be friends after always being treated like he was second class.

Near the end of the semester, Willy and his team won a game, causing someone from the other team to pick a fight with Willy after the game, resulting in a concussion for the other guy. Willy pulled a knife on him, threatening him until campus security joined in to stop it, along with witnesses to the fight.

Willy was charged with assault and carrying a concealed weapon on campus, then was kicked out of school. Before the end of the semester he arrived home, disappointed. After coming back home, he managed to get a job in an auto shop where he stayed for nine years. He couldn't care less about going back to school and decided to just make a living in his hometown.

In 1951 he started a gang, a greaser clique. It consisted of six members; Willy, Elmer, Freddie, Tyrone, Lou and Ollie. Willy became the non-official leader of the group, making most of the huge decisions, like on October 21, 1953, when he took his group and crashed a high school dance. When they first started their clique Willy was 21 years old, Elmer 22, Freddie 19, Tyrone 23, Lou 21, and Ollie 16. They were still young enough to blend in to get into the school dance, but as soon as they were caught, they called the police. Willy and his gang bailed.

Throughout 1954, there was a lot of drag racing going on out on the highway near the lake. Willy and his crew would often attend these races and many times won. One day someone ratted them out to the police. On the night of September 6, someone notified them that they had seen cop cars heading their way so they all left.

The next morning someone was reported missing from the lake. His name was Greg Sherman. His parents told the police that he never came home that night, and the last time he was seen was at that race. Tracy, his girlfriend and Willy's old high school crush, said she wasn't with him that night, but was sure that "demons" got him. Everyone thought she was demented when she said that, but she still held to her claim. Greg's parents blamed her for their son's disappearance and wanted to file a restraining order.

Tracy didn't have many friends, especially after the incident, but when Willy heard about what happened and that she still lived in town, he went to visit her.

She was glad to see him. She asked what he had done since they graduated, so he explained to her about him going to college, how he was kicked out, and that he just decided to move back home. He didn't bother to ask about her boyfriend, but did seem to know something when she mentioned demons. Growing up, Willy never once visited the lake, nor would his father ever allow it.

In 1955, Willy and Tracy started to date and had their first kiss in the summer. Many times he'd take her to the soda shop along with his friends and they would dance to rock and roll. On the night of October 27, after everyone left, Willy and Elmer took off together to watch a movie called *Rebel Without a Cause* at the local theatre. After the show, they followed a man as he exited the theatre. Once he had had gotten just two blocks from his house, Willy and Elmer jumped and mugged him.

They soon called for an ambulance. Willy had a master plan that would involve humiliating him when they were brought in for questioning. The plan was for Willy to leave before the cops arrived, then appear like just another civilian when he came to the station as a witness to protest the man's claims about what he might say about Elmer. Willy was able to put on a very good act, and they appeared to have known the man was on probation.

The man's name was Kent Burkett, and he was once charged for sexual assault on his ex-girlfriend. Willy and Elmer knew that this man was their perfect target. Willy told a fake story to the cops about Kent, saying that Willy was walking home from the theatre when someone unexpectedly tried to jump Elmer. This led to Kent almost killing Elmer with a knife that Willy had planted in his jacket. Suddenly, Willy came along to help Elmer by attacking the mugger with his bare hands. There was another witness in the area at the time when this happened who was brought into the station to testify, although it was actually Tyrone, pretending to be another witness.

The following week, a trial was held in the town's courtroom. With the story told and everyone believing that Kent had broken his probation, he was sent to prison for three years with a $2,000 fine. Only Willy's crew knew the true story, but feared to come clean because of their involvement. They continued on with their lives and kept going back to the soda shop to party; all but Elmer, who didn't go because he couldn't stand to look at Willy anymore.

Starting that night, Elmer began to resent Willy, and Tracy even began to feel apprehensive toward what happened that night. She would sometimes try to ask his friends what really happened but they just stayed quiet. She began to befriend the youngest, Ollie, more and knew that he was the more pleasant one. Whenever she wasn't with Willy, she hung out with Ollie. Lou was also very friendly and would sometimes join them. Although Ollie was more approachable and honest, he couldn't tell her what happened that night since he wasn't there, and no one in his crew would tell him. Even Lou wouldn't tell him, even though he and Ollie were best pals.

By the next year in 1956, Tracy asked Ollie to come to the shop with her, but he feared that if Willy was there and saw them coming in together he'd kill him. But she insisted and he eventually agreed. As they walked in through the front door together, Freddie showed up. He stopped when he saw them come in, then wandered off. Ollie and Tracy found a booth and ordered two milkshakes.

Tracy liked Ollie and thought he was wonderful to talk to, unlike Willy. She got up from the booth to put a coin in the jukebox, then ran back to Ollie, pulling him out of his seat to dance with her.

Everyone soon got up to follow and it turned into a dance floor with all different moves; the twist, hand jive, bop and cha-cha. They all enjoyed the music.

Within the hour Willy showed up, along with Freddie and Tyrone. When Willy saw the two of them dancing, he heatedly walked over to ask what they were doing. Tracy asked Willy to calm down and told him that they were just dancing, but Willy was paranoid about losing her, and just stared at them, believing it was more than that. He grabbed Tracy by her left arm and tried to forcefully take her outside and back home. Ollie put his hand on Willy's shoulder, yelling, "Leave her alone! You're hurting her!"

Willy let go of Tracy, then turned to face Ollie, taunting him. Ollie was scared to confront Willy like this, but still insisted that he leave her alone. Willy looked at Freddie and Tyrone with embarrassment, then turned back to Ollie, laughing and shoving him with both hands. As soon as Ollie tried to say something, Willy punched him. Everyone stopped dancing and looked over to what was happening. Willy forcefully told Ollie that he was now out of the gang, and took off with Freddie and Tyrone following, leaving Tracy behind.

Later, Ollie met up with Lou and told him that Willy had kicked him out. Lou told Ollie that he informed the rest of the gang that he too was out because he was moving to Missouri and wouldn't see them again. Before Lou left, Ollie told him farewell and that he hoped he'd see him again.

Shortly after the incident, Willy and Tracy broke up, and Elmer was arrested for armed robbery, which meant only three were left in the gang.

Ollie went to visit Tracy at her house but saw her kissing Willy through the window as if they had gotten back together so he walked away and let them be. Willy then gave Tracy a promise ring, showing her that he would one day ask her to marry him.

The next morning, Ollie woke up feeling empty, knowing that he was no longer in a group, that he had no friends, and the girl that he liked was back together with her jerk boyfriend, so he decided he would go and try to find a job.

Two years later, in 1958, Willy was getting close to asking Tracy to marry him, then one day someone appeared. He was stalking Willy and Tracy after he saw them together at the soda shop. After Willy and Tracy left, he followed them to the hockey rink. Someone had left the door open so they snuck in to have some quiet time. When the rink employee came back in, they hid until he left. Finally the door shut and they had the rink to themselves.

What they didn't know was that the person who followed them from the soda shop was in there with them. He had hid, planning to attack them in the rink without anyone there to catch him in the act. Willy and Tracy sat on the bleachers, kissing and talking romantically to each other, then Willy took her out onto the ice. They began to get closer to each other, standing in the center of the rink. Willy looked passionately into her eyes as he got down on one knee, getting ready to propose. Tracy looked down at him with glee, looking around the big clearing on the ice as if it was happening in public. As Willy began to say the words, they heard the door open. The man exited out the front of the rink, then began to run after Willy saw him.

Willy was furious that someone had been watching them and ruined such a great moment, and he began to chase after the mysterious person, losing him once he got outside. Tracy calmed Willy down, telling him not to worry or let them ruin their special day. Soon after, Willy took her to get coffee. After they got to Willy's house, he became more disappointed about how his perfect moment was ruined, and punched a dent in his door. He called Freddie and Tyrone to come to his house so they could hang out the rest of the night. When Tracy left the room he told them how he was so close to proposing until some perverted son-of-a-bitch interrupted him.

They told Willy that if they were there, they would have trashed him, but to drop it and change the mood, the trio, along with Tracy, headed to Freddie's house to drink and eat pizza. Even Elmer showed up. Willy asked where he had been and Elmer admitted that he was mad at Willy for the prank they pulled on the man a few years ago, but he knew he himself had to take some of the blame since he was part of it.

They all took shots and all but Willy got wasted. Often you hear stories of people who have made their biggest mistakes after getting drunk and regretting it later on, so when they decided to go for a ride, Willy drove since he was the only one sober.

Freddie let Willy drive his car out to the high school where they were planning to break in and perhaps drink more. Willy parked the car out on the staff parking lot and they all got out of the car and started breaking windows on the front doors of the school. They made their way down to the gymnasium and started dancing to some loud music. Willy and Tracy were dancing, Freddie and Tyrone were drinking on the bleachers, and Elmer found a basketball and was shooting some hoops. Suddenly the music stopped. Willy asked Elmer to turn it back on, but Elmer told him it wasn't him that turned it off. Freddie and Tyrone went to see what was happening. They found that the music had been turned off, meaning someone else was in there with them. Freddie and Tyrone drunkenly made their way back to Willy to tell him that someone else was there.

Willy wondered if it could be the same guy who stalked him and Tracy at the rink, so he ordered the guys to find him while he stayed with Tracy. Freddie went down the hall to the office and cafeteria, Tyrone searched the science wing, and Elmer went down to where they broke in, which was close to the library.

Elmer walked down the stairs into the library and passed the non-fiction section. Instead of looking for the guy following them, he pulled out an old book he had read when he was in high school and sat down, leaning against the wall at the end of the narrow section. A few minutes later he heard someone else enter the library. He immediately closed the book and put it back into the empty slot, walking out to see who it was, assuming it was one of his friends.

After walking out, turning to his left and looking up the stairs, Elmer saw someone looking down at him with a gun. With a stiff body, anger in his eyes, and an empty feeling felt while holding onto the gun, the man was tempted to do the first thing he had thought of before his arrest; the arrest for assault following the fabricated story... It was Kent Burkett.

Kent and Elmer said nothing, just looked at each other until Elmer finally tried to say he was sorry. Kent informed him that his life was ruined because of him and Willy, and for that he was going to take their lives. Elmer tried to calm him down, telling him that if he killed him he would regret it for the rest of his life and he'd just go back to jail. Kent told him that he didn't care and that he wasn't afraid of dying either. Since the lie, he had no family, no wife, nothing. Now, the only thing he really had left was his revenge.

The single shot alerted the others and they ran to where the sound came from. Freddie and Tyrone found each other and made their way down the echoing hallway toward the gymnasium to meet Willy and Tracy. The couple came out and saw the two of them. Willy told them to stay together and to be careful since the attacker had a gun. They all looked for Elmer, but couldn't find him. Since they had already covered most of the remaining ground, they scurried over to the library. Freddie begged Willy to leave since the man had a gun, but Willy insisted that they find Elmer first.

The group soon came upon Elmer's body. He had been shot in the head, right between the eyes. Freddie again begged for them to leave now that they knew Elmer was dead, but Willy was focused, observing everything around him until he got a glimpse of a man hiding upstairs. Willy looked back at them and mouthed for them to run, meaning he knew the attacker was in there. They all ran to the door with Freddie being the first one out. Before Willy could get out, Kent fired at him. Willy quickly got behind the librarian's desk and crouched down. Kent held the gun focused at the desk, moving forward.

Willy looked behind him and saw a guillotine paper cutter. He made his way over to the paper cutter and quickly unscrewed the blade to use as a weapon. When Kent reached the desk, he looked over it with the gun pointed, but didn't find Willy, so he crept behind it to get a closer look. He was surprised when Willy popped out from behind the photocopier. The arm Kent was leading with and holding the gun with was battered when Willy took a swing downward, gashing his arm. Kent was pulled down with the cutter, dropping the gun. His injured right arm was too weak to grab the gun so he tried to grab it with his left. Willy pushed him back with the cutter by placing his hands on each end of the blade, pressing it across Kent's chest and thrusting forward. Kent's back slammed against the desk and Willy grabbed the gun and pointed it at Kent.

Willy taunted him, letting Kent know how mad he was that he had killed his friend. Kent told him the same thing he told Elmer – that he now had no friends – and Willy admitted it was his fault this had happened. He knew that he couldn't possibly tell Elmer he was sorry since it wouldn't matter anymore, and knew he had to finish what he had started – by pulling the trigger. The rest of the group ran in and they could easily see what was going on when they saw Kent's face. They all looked at Willy helplessly, scared, not knowing what they were going to do.

The next morning, the police investigation began when they discovered someone had broken into the high school. A funeral was arranged for Elmer, but Willy had already taken care of Kent's body by disposing of it in a place no one would ever go.

About three weeks after the incident, just when they thought they could put it all behind them, Freddie and Tyrone were thinking of turning Willy in. They didn't want to cover him anymore and didn't want to have any part of killing people. They talked to Tracy about their fears and she said she would go along with it, but instead went to warn Willy what they were planning to do. He knew he was going to have to leave. He asked her to come with him but she couldn't be a fugitive too, so she stayed. He swore that one day he'd come back and marry her as he promised.

Later that night, Willy packed his things and left town. He took one last drive down the street looking at everything, including his father's shop, Snider's Cuts. He drove from Montana into Washington State where he decided to join the Army.

The rest of the year Willy spent training at boot camp until finally, in early 1959, he was sent to Vietnam. He and the rest of his platoon were brought to the military airbase Chu Lai. They headed to the barracks and were greeted by their commander, Lieutenant Riggs. They saluted him as he walked by, examining his new soldiers. He could see in Willy's eyes that he already had that thousand yard stare, but continued his inspection.

Willy was soon befriended by one of his comrades, Jimmy from Philadelphia. The platoon called him Jimmy from Philly. Willy told Jimmy he joined the Army for the benefits. Jimmy told him he joined so he could serve his country, and in return earn some money for him and his fiancée back home.

This made Willy more eager to do his part and return home to marry the love of his life – after him being guilty of murder blew over. It took a while for Willy and his platoon to be called for active duty so they remained at the base for four months.

On April 9, Lieutenant Riggs received orders to take his men deep into the jungle to retrieve anyone, dead or alive, after receiving word that there had been an ambush up north. Heading up near the DMZ, close to northern Vietnam, they travelled for eight days.

One night Jimmy came to Willy and asked him if they could try leaning their backs against each other while sleeping so they wouldn't have lie with their heads in the mud, which they continued to do whenever they could.

They arrived at their location, finding a huge

clearing where it was obvious the group had had serious gunfights. They found that no one had survived. They soon realized it was necessary to now save themselves when the first shot was fired, killing one of Lieutenant Riggs' men. They quickly took cover and fired back at the enemy.

Willy separated from the group, with Jimmy by his side. They crouched down, moving slowly toward where the enemy was hiding. Willy saw one up ahead and told Jimmy to stay hidden while he took care of him. Jimmy hid behind a big bush while Willy crawled over to the man without the enemy's allies being able to see him. Willy rose up behind him, pulling him down by placing his left hand over his mouth, and stabbing the man in the stomach with the other. After the man was silenced and placed quietly on the ground, Willy removed his hand once the man's eyes closed and his body turned motionless. Willy signaled Jimmy to approach and stay low. When Jimmy crawled up, he was jolted at the sight of the dead corpse.

They saw three more enemies in a group together. Willy decided that Jimmy should go after the one that had separated from the others while Willy went after the other two. They hid and, after seeing the first two pass, Willy sent Jimmy after the third. Willy snuck up behind the two men while they were under cover, firing at the platoon. He again took out his knife and brought it down on the man's left side, plunging it into the back of his spine, killing him instantly. The other man looked over and tried to shoot Willy, but Willy stopped him by grabbing the gun and pushing it away. He got up behind him, grabbing him by the hair and smashing his head multiple times into the log where they were taking cover.

Jimmy seemed to be biding his time with the man he was following. He raised his gun from his hiding place, hesitating to pull the trigger. All he could think of was the sight of the man Willy had killed. When the man turned, Jimmy got down, staying quiet and motionless. The man started walking toward where Willy had killed the first man, then started running back to the larger group where it was more safe. Before he reached the group, Willy shot him through the neck. The man fell dead, and Jimmy rose from his hiding place to show himself. A loud boom was heard, the shot of a bazooka fired from one of the men in Willy's platoon. That flushed out the enemy, and Willy's platoon began to move forward with the enemy now under suppressed fire. The enemy became overwhelmed and what was left of them began to retreat.

When their mission was completed, they collected their dead. The Vietcongs were left there to rot, just as they did when they ambushed their men before Willy's platoon got there. The deceased Americans would be brought back to the military base in the U.S.... to go home.

The following night, Jimmy told Willy that he didn't kill a single man that day. Willy told him that he would have plenty of chances and that it would be a hard thing to do since it felt horrible to first kill a man. Jimmy again asked why Willy was there since everyone had a purpose for joining the Army. Willy told him that he had no purpose, but he was running away. Willy shared with him his secret about being a con artist, and that he had started rumors about a man that sent him to prison and ruined his life. He also told him that he had wrecked everything for him, his friends and his girl, and that joining the Army was a way for him to get away from things until he could return. Jimmy felt disturbed by his story but decided to keep it to himself so things would go smoothly with Willy.

The lieutenant was pleased to hear how well Willy fought that day and began to have faith in him. As soon as they returned to base, he was promoted to Private First Class. About four weeks later, Willy was ordered to lead a few men into the jungle to search for a group of soldiers whose helicopter had been shot down eleven miles out from their home base.

As if moving through the jungle with the scorching sun burning red marks at the back of their necks and biting parasites in the jungle was not bad enough, it became worse when they found the chopper, along with its dead crew. Willy ordered them to retrieve anything and anyone they could find. One, however, separated from the group and wandered off into the jungle. He sat down against a tree, raising his arm to his forehead to wipe off the sweat, then heard hissing sounds above him. He looked up to see that it was a snake, but for some reason he was not startled by it. Instead, he was intrigued by the snake and let it slither around his shoulder when it came down. Soon after though, he heard snarls coming from behind the tree. He got up with his gun, with the snake still on his shoulders. He snuck over to where the sound came from and Willy, noticing that one of the soldiers was missing, went to search for him while the rest of his crew retrieved anything they could find from the chopper.

The soldier came upon a dead body, which looked like could have been one of the dead soldiers from the chopper, but he couldn't figure out what had made that noise and how the body got this far from the chopper. He figured that he either fell out before it crashed or was dragged out. The second idea crossed his mind again when he heard another snarl and something moving around him in the trees. With his heart rate rising, sweat running down his right cheek, and not willing to move from the clearing, he became oblivious as to what he should do.

Suddenly, right behind him, what had made the snarl appeared – it was a tiger. It was on top of him as he was faced down, then he rolled over with the tiger still on top of him. He tried to get it off by grabbing it by the neck and twisting its head but the tiger was too strong. Its mouth moved closer and closer, trying to bite him, scratching him badly down his left arm.

At that moment, the soldier was saved by both Willy and the snake as the snake bit down on the tiger's right paw, making the tiger jerk its head up, howling in pain. A shot then rang out as the tiger was shot through the head by Willy. Willy quickly came over to help the soldier up and asked what he was doing drifting away from the group. The soldier admitted that he had no real reason and apologized for his ignorance. Willy threatened him, telling him that if he wandered off from the group again, he'd find and kill him himself.

Willy then saw the snake and was about to shoot it when the soldier stopped him and asked him not to shoot it, but let him take it back to base. Willy thought he was odd for asking but could care less when the soldier told him that the snake had saved his life. They headed back with the snake on the soldier's shoulders. Everyone laughed at him on the journey back, and again back at the base.

Once they arrived back at base, Willy asked the

soldier his name, and he told him that it was Fuller. He mentioned to Willy that he had given the snake a name, Moses.

Later that evening Willy met up with Jimmy and another soldier fighting the war, Dean. He asked to join in and when he did, the three talked about his mission that day. He told them that they had found the crashed chopper, along with the crew's dead bodies, and that one of the guys on his mission was attacked by a tiger but he had saved him.

Willy thought about last time, how there were no survivors again, and that they would just have to bring bodies back to base to be sent home to their families. He was just glad he wouldn't have to be the messenger. He could only imagine what it would be like to die in that war, with no family or friends who would attend his funeral. He knew that there was a good chance that he was going to die and he didn't care where it would be since he probably deserved it. Even though that was the case, he didn't forget about Tracy and hoped he would return home to marry her after his service was done.

Two years later, in 1962, Willy had gone on several combat missions in Vietnam. He was promoted to Sergeant during that time and formed his own attack squad which included himself, Jimmy, Dean, Fuller, and two others, Ian and Giuseppe. With Willy as their leader, Jimmy their communications specialist, Dean their engineering and explosives expert, Fuller their sharpshooter, Ian their medic, and Giuseppe their weapons specialist, they served well together. Willy decided that it was now time for him to return home and be with his love.

On March 12, Willy returned to Roarke. The first person he went to see was Tracy. He went by her house to see if she was there, and it seemed like her parents had left her the house years earlier. He would soon find out that it did not just belong to her, but her new husband too.

As he walked up her driveway to the front door, he could see through the window of the door; his girlfriend was kissing another man in the kitchen. He dropped the hand he was just about to knock with, and put both hands on the door, leaning against it with his head down in grief. He moved away from the door forcefully and walked down her driveway, throwing her engagement ring into their garbage can.

Since he was done with Tracy, he went to go see his father, not knowing that his father was already dead. He came to his father's house which was now the residence of a different family, then tried the shop to see if he was there. He found that the shop was no longer in business.

He did manage to meet Ollie when another store caught Willy's attention; that store was Ollie's. He walked inside and approached the clerk to ask who the owner was. The clerk told him the owner's name was Ollie Fonzerelli. Willy asked to see him and it was his old friend. Ollie was shocked to see Willy like this since everyone thought Willy was dead or had run off somewhere, never to be seen again after the events that occurred a few years ago.

They started catching up, asking each other questions about what had gone on the last few years. Willy told him that he had run off and joined the Army to get away from his trouble and that when he came back, he found out Tracy was with someone else even though he promised to return to her.

Ollie told Willy that Tracy had fallen in love with this man and just didn't have those feelings for him anymore. He also told Willy about him opening his shop just last year. Ollie didn't know much about what happened to Freddie and Tyrone, nor Lou, guessing he was probably still in Missouri. But what Willy really wanted to know is what happened to his father. Ollie was afraid to look him in the eye and tell him the truth, but he deserved to know since it was his dad. Willy's father had died of a heart attack just nine months after Willy left Roarke.

Willy was absolutely devastated to hear this news

and decided to leave, but before he left he apologized to Ollie, telling him that he probably didn't deserve his forgiveness, but Ollie still reconciled with him. People thought Willy was dead, so he thought he should keep it that way since he no longer had a home there.

Soon after, Willy decided to go back into the Army. He felt that there was nothing left for him in Roarke, so he decided to go back to Vietnam and keep fighting. He returned to base to meet up with his team and again took command.

From 1963 - 1965, Willy and the rest of the platoon were led by Lieutenant Riggs and were stationed up north to set up base. They were ordered to never leave their post unless relieved from duty. On May 11, 1964, Lieutenant Riggs ordered Willy to lead his strike team on a mission to find and rescue P.O.W.s from a nearby camp.

Willy and his crew geared up and made their way to the camp. When they got there, Willy ordered Jimmy to scout ahead around the area to find the prisoners. Giuseppe criticized Willy, saying he was a fool to send in a coward who had barely pulled the trigger since he joined the Army. Ian told him to shut up and that he was the fool. Willy told them both to shut up or the enemy was going to hear them. Willy had Fuller hiding nearby to cover them with his sniper gun in case anyone was chasing them while they rescued the prisoners.

Jimmy kept moving, then came to a guarded cage. Jimmy crept over behind a tree, whistling to lure the guard in his direction. The guard walked over, thinking it was a bird in the tree, but with a surprise attack Jimmy quickly subdued him by putting his left hand over his head and finished him off by slitting his throat. He grabbed the key, let the prisoners out, and they headed back to Willy and the others. They couldn't move well because they were half-dead due to their wounds and starvation.

They tried to make a quick pace but the prisoner's injuries were slowing them down. A guard came to the cage to find the prisoners missing and rushed to alert the others. Their commander ordered them to head out and find the escaped prisoners and whoever helped them break out. Willy's group could hear shouts and whistles from the camp once they got about six-hundred feet away. With the prisoner's injuries slowing them down, the enemy was able to catch up. Willy and his men hid while a group of forty Vietcong's passed them, heading down toward Lieutenant Riggs' camp. Willy radioed to him that they were coming, but before Willy and his group could move out, there were four more men who didn't know Willy and his men were hiding. As they entered through the trees, Giuseppe went after them.

Willy and the others didn't see him leave their group. The Vietcong soldiers separated into two-man groups, with Giuseppe going after the first two. He grabbed the one in back from behind with a piece of wire, wrapping it around the man's neck, pulling him down and quietly killing him. The other man stopped, looking behind him only to not see his partner. He became scared, but before he could call out for help, Giuseppe circled him, pulling him down, snapping his neck, and killing him.

Before he could head out for another group, Fuller killed the Vietcongs with a single shot. He was hiding at least 112 metres away and shot them with his sniper gun, the bullet going through one man's head then penetrating the other's. Celebrating his perfect shot, he spoke to Moses as the snake was hanging on his shoulder, "Two birds with one bullet, Moses."

Willy was furious that Giuseppe had separated from the group but despite his frustration, the team gathered to make their way back to camp. When they arrived, they found a battle was going on. The camp was in flames as Willy and his crew rushed in to join the fight. While Lieutenant Riggs and his men were fighting in the camp, Willy flanked the enemy by pulling them away to the west side of the base while Lieutenant Riggs and his men fought them on the east side.

After realizing they were being attacked from both sides, the Vietcong soldiers were forced to retreat, but before the battle was over, Lieutenant Riggs was surrounded by Vietcong with nowhere to run. He quickly grabbed one of them as a human shield, shooting two more in front of him, followed by two shots to the back of the soldier he had been using to shield himself. The Vietcong captain came up from behind and shot him through his left lung. When the captain heard Willy and his crew approaching, he ran.

When Willy came to the lieutenant, he looked at his wound and then looked farther out, seeing a man running before he escaped into the jungle. The captain stopped and looked back, proud that he killed the lieutenant, then disappeared into the jungle.

The lieutenant woke up, breathing heavily, knowing he was dying. He told Willy that he was the greatest soldier he had ever seen. Before he died the Lieutenant smiled, knowing that he died with honor and bravery.

Six hours later, two helicopters arrived. In one was Colonel Harrison, there to see if the mission was complete and take back any casualties. Colonel Harrison asked who was in charge, so Willy told him that he was now that their lieutenant was dead. The colonel was a great friend of the lieutenant and was very sorry that he had been killed.

A few weeks after Lieutenant Riggs and the rest of the deceased were brought back home and buried, Willy and his crew were brought to Washington to meet President Lyndon B. Johnson. Each received a Congressional Medal of Honor for their heroic deeds throughout the war. After the presentation, Willy spoke to Colonel Harrison, who wanted to congratulate him. The colonel told him that he had heard many great things about him since he first served in Lieutenant Riggs' platoon. Since Willy was his right-hand man and had been granted this medal of valor, the colonel awarded him with Lieutenant Riggs' command as the new lieutenant. Willy accepted and was called back to Vietnam in less than a week.

For five more years, Willy and his platoon patrolled the border to protect the south from any attacks. There were other missions to search, fight and rescue, but one in particular was to find one Vietcong named Captain An. He was notorious for killing so many Americans. In Vietnamese, An means peaceful, but not to the Americans.

On August 18, 1969, Willy finally found the captain's location. He was hiding in a village called Ha Tinh. It was not a large town and Willy's platoon would outnumber them. Willy got all his men to circle and flank the camp so no one would escape. Willy ordered his soldiers not to harm any civilians. As they went in for the attack, the villagers panicked and the ones with guns came out to fight. While Willy's men were handling the threat outside, Willy took five more inside An's palace. As they moved down the hallways, another gunfight began between Willy's men and An's guards. Willy managed to kill three and left the others for his men to handle while he made his way down to An's office. Willy went inside and closed the door behind him, looking around but An wasn't there.

When Willy walked past a closet, An popped out and grabbed Willy's gun before he could raise it. Willy tried to get a hold of An but dropped the gun in the struggle. An pulled out his knife and started to attack Willy, but Willy grabbed his arm and pushed him against the wall. As he pushed him, he looked closely at his face and could see that he was the captain that had killed Lieutenant Riggs.

An also recognized Willy from that day. Willy became angry and threw An onto his desk, telling An that he was going to pay for what he had done to Lieutenant Riggs, and Willy knew he understood English. An came at Willy with his knife, and Willy moved his head to the left, dodging his attack, following it with a left hook to An's face. An dropped his knife and Willy moved forward with another punch, but An met him with a spinning kick. Willy fell to the ground but quickly got back up. Knives in hand, they evaded each other's attacks whenever they made a move. Soon they got close to each other, grabbing each other, then An pushed Willy to the ground. He started to swing down at Willy with his knife but before he could, Willy grabbed his knife at the tip of the blade and threw it at An, penetrating the center of his chest. Willy got up and walked over to watch him die as he slowly collapsed to the ground.

Willy and his platoon were victorious that day, and Willy was promoted to Captain. In late 1970, Willy retired. He'd had enough of war. He believed that he should've died in Vietnam rather than back at home, but after his service was up, he gave his team a farewell.

Returning home, he slowly became an eccentric old man that lived at the lake, until he finally had a change of heart when he met a boy named Victor.

Chapter Six

As morning approached, Victor, David, Steven and Ollie gathered the dead bodies of the werewolves. It was a problem as the creatures had turned back into humans after they died. Meanwhile, they had no family so they had to get rid of them before the police became suspicious.

Victor and his dad searched for the man the werewolves had attacked that night. They started at the man's car which was really smashed on the outside, finding blood on the road. David looked into the car and found the man's wallet. He looked inside for his identification, and it said his name was Jim Unger. Victor began to wonder if he was possibly his cooking teacher's husband. They started looking for him by following a trail of blood into an alley. As they came further down the alley, they saw legs poking out from the other side of a garbage can. Victor walked toward it and saw the man who appeared to be dead. As he looked closer at him, the man opened his eyes. Victor backed away surprised and asked, "Are you okay?"

The man was breathing heavily and said, "Tell my

wife I love her."

He fell silent and Victor felt sorry for him. He started to blame himself for bringing the werewolves here. "Dad, it's my fault. If I hadn't gone to that house, this man wouldn't be dead."

"Victor, it's not your fault. You should know how proud I am of you. You fought hard last night to keep yourself and the others safe, and there's no one else who could've done that."

"How am I going to tell his wife, my teacher, that her husband died?"

"Alright… look, here's how it's going to be. You're going to go up to her and tell her that it was a car accident. No one will bat an eye if you say that."

"What about Reggie? What are we going to tell people about what happened to him?"

"I guess I could get Ollie to convince everyone that Reggie was on his way home from work, and while walking across the street the driver accidentally hit him and Reggie didn't stand a chance."

David called the police and reported two dead bodies, and it wasn't long before they came to investigate. They asked him a few questions as to what he saw, heard and what he was doing that night. David said, "I was closing up my shop to go home and see my family but when I turned around I saw a car speeding down the road. I yelled out to the man crossing to look out, but it was too late."

The police officers believed him, and had the bodies taken away in an ambulance to the nearest hospital. Around 8:00 a.m. Victor went to school and met up with Steven. Steven didn't say much in Socials, but when they got to Cooking class, Ms. Unger was not there to teach class. This was a hint that she may have already been told about her husband. At the end of classes, Victor went down the hall to the front door and out of the school where he waited for his mother to pick him up. Steven caught up and asked, "So, what are you going to do?"

"Well, I'm just waiting for my mom to pick me up and go home."

"I mean, what are you going to do about what happened last night?"

"I don't know, what am I supposed to do? We should be happy we're alive."

"So you're just not going to do anything?"

"Look, what do you want from me? You saw

those things last night and surely you don't plan on going near them again!"

"You brought them here. People died because of you and no one knows except you. We have to do something and whether you like it or not, I'm part of this too."

"Even if it is my fault, I don't want you to get hurt too, now goodbye."

Victor's mom drove by to pick him up and when he got inside they drove away, leaving Steven to just watch them drive away down the street. He still felt like he should do something but walked away, heading home.

Victor was happy that Steven wanted to help because that showed him that Steven actually cared for him. Back in Seattle when he tried to make new friends, people just ignored him. The only friends he had were the ones he met when he was very little. For the first time when someone actually wanted to be his friend, he told him off – but only because he didn't want anyone else getting killed because of his doing.

Victor's mom said nothing in the car, her face was straight. Victor couldn't tell if she was focusing on the road or worried about tonight. "Mom, are we staying in a hotel tonight?"

"I don't know. I don't know what your father has planned."

As they came to the shop, Victor walked into his dad's office and said, "Hi, Dad."

"Hi, son. How was school?"

"Well, it's tough knowing that you wrecked a woman's life," Victor replied gloomily.

"Well, don't worry about dressing up for a funeral because we're leaving town today."

"What are you talking about?"

"I'm talking about us moving to ensure our safety. I don't want us to have to go through what we did last night ever again. People died, and we nearly did too. It was bad enough making up lies about what happened to those people."

"But Dad, we can't leave, it's not right."

"What's right is keeping my family safe."

"I'm not leaving! I feel guilty for what happened and there's no way I'm running away from this!"

"Victor, I make the calls here and by tonight we'll

be out of Montana and start our lives somewhere else! You kids made big fucking mistakes and as a father, I'm forced to take desperate measures! Now go see Mom because this discussion is over!"

Before Victor could leave, he looked at his father, eager to say something else but before he could his father yelled, "NOW!"

Victor walked out very furious, walking past his mother outside the door. Susan followed him and watched him walk away down the sidewalk shouting, "Victor!"

He didn't answer. Victor understood what his dad was trying to tell him, but what he didn't realize was that there was more at stake than just themselves. If they left the town behind and never told anyone what had been happening, especially since they wouldn't believe them, Victor would regret it for the rest of his life.

At the hospital, Ms. Unger went to see the deceased body of her husband. When the doctor asked her to get a closer look at him, he showed her that the injuries were really teeth and claw marks. The doctor said, "Ms. Unger, I don't think your husband was killed by a car crash. You see these marks on the upper torso and down the spine? Well, it looks like he was clawed to death, not to mention this mark on his right shoulder. It looks like an animal bite."

"But what kind of an animal could do this?"

"My guess is it was a wolf, but I know this was no car accident."

As Victor walked down the street, he saw five men with guns and overheard them saying they were going out to the lake to hunt and camp. They got into their truck and drove away. Victor continued walking and came across an arcade, seeing Steven inside. Victor walked up to the game he was playing and said, "Alright, Steven."

Steven looked at him puzzled asking, "Alright, what?"

"I want you to come with me tonight and finish this."

"I thought you didn't want me to help you. What about your family?"

"I couldn't convince my dad to stay, so I want you on my side as we kill these things once and for all."

"What are your parents going to think about this?"

"It's best they don't know."

"Okay, well what do you suggest? I mean… you were right, we can't do this. It's suicide and it's best we stay away from it."

"No, you were right. We're the only ones that know, and I'm responsible so I'm going down there. That is, if you'll join me."

Steven was scared to say yes but he knew if he didn't help Victor, he would consider himself as a coward and a false friend. He agreed, "Alright I'll go, but what do I take with me?"

Anything big or perhaps utensils made out of silver. There's just one problem. My family and I are leaving town, so I'll have to come up with a plan. Is there a gas station on the road out of town?"

"Yes, there's one but its thirty miles out."

"Okay well, when my family and I get there, I'm going to drive back into town so they can't stop us. But we must keep this a secret or it'll ruin everything."

"Victor, aren't you scared at all?"

"Of course I am. Why wouldn't I be?"

"Well, because what you did last night was amazing. I mean, you killed both those werewolves. You just fended them off and I probably would've been dead if you weren't there beside me."

"That's nice but I don't want praise, I just want this to be over soon. Before we step onto their territory, they're going to know we're coming, so we have to be careful and watch out for any surprise attack they might have."

"Let's meet right here at six," said Steven.

After their discussion, Victor and Steven walked away, planning to stick to the plan. As Victor walked back, he wondered what it was going to be like in the future. He didn't want his parents to be mad at him for turning against them, but he would rather have that than to move to another town, just hoping that everything would be better.

When Victor got back to the shop his mother asked, "Where were you?"

"I had to take a walk."

"Well, we're going to be leaving soon, so stay here."

David had the store closed and Victor went over

to sit in one of the chairs. Natalie walked over and sat in the one next to him. For once she was being nice to Victor when she asked, "Are you okay?"

Victor kept looking at the mirror in front of him and answered, "I'm fine but I'm not letting this go. I have to deal with this and I have to do it tonight!"

"What are you saying? You're not actually going to go up against those things are you?"

"Yes Natalie, it has to be done."

"But what about Mom and Dad?"

"What about them?"

"They won't let you do this, Victor."

Victor responded, looking over his right shoulder at Natalie and said, "Well, then they don't need to know. Tonight I'm going to that house with Steven and we're going to kill them."

"I don't want you to get hurt. You're my brother and I love you."

"Natalie, I know you're afraid. I know you're afraid of losing me, you're afraid that if I die that makes you responsible and that one day your heart will die too when you're alone after Mom and Dad are gone. But I promise you that's not going to happen. What I know is that the farther you run, the harder is it to accept what is left behind. We disappoint, we disappear, we die, but I need you on my side on this, which is to keep it to yourself and don't tell Mom and Dad."

Victor's words touched Natalie and she knew that somehow he was on his game so she asked, "What exactly are you going to do? We're leaving soon."

"When we get to the next gas station on the road, I'm going to take the car back to town and meet up with Steven. I don't like going behind Mom and Dad's backs, but ultimately I have to do this."

This was really starting to make Natalie more concerned for her brother and she wished that none of this had happened. "Victor, why did you walk to that house yesterday? None of this would have happened if you had done what Willy told you to do."

"Oh... so now you care what Willy says or believes. You know something Natalie, you didn't make fun of Willy behind his back because of who he is, but because you're one of those people who always likes to talk about people to look better and get respect. You are so judgmental that you've become such a hypocrite. Like me, for example. I hardly do anything.

Growing up, I haven't smoked, drank, stayed out past my curfew, I don't do badly in school, or talk trash about people. I've always kept to myself, and yet you still call me on the spot like you can read my mind. You've always just been so awkward to be around that it's always made me nervous. I just can't stand being near you anymore."

Victor got up and saw his dad walking in as he said, "Come on, we're leaving now. Everyone, in the car."

Natalie felt extremely sad about what Victor said, but kept her word and didn't say anything.

As David was driving, he could see through the rearview mirror that Victor was still upset about them leaving. Natalie asked David, "So Dad, who's going to run the shop now?"

"I don't know but I told my co-worker that I had to leave because of my daughter. I'm sorry that I had to involve you, Natalie. I told them that I had to travel with you so you wouldn't be alone going off to school."

"Dad, come on, you really had to say that?"

"Yes, I mean, they wouldn't believe me if I told them the real reason." They drove to their house very frightened, as they wanted to quickly gather their things and be on their way. It took them about half an hour, much faster than when they moved in. All the furniture was put in the carrier attached to the back of the car.

When they were done packing, they got into the car and started down the highway. They didn't know where they were going to go, they just wanted to get as far away as they possibly could.

Victor stuck to his plan. When they got to the gas station that Steven had told him about, they all got out. Victor's heart was beating fast, as he was nervous to perform the most rebellious thing he had ever done. Natalie and Susan went inside to buy snacks, and David stayed outside to pump the car with gas. Victor stood away from the side of the car where his dad was pumping the gas and went to the driver's side. The keys were inside, so Victor got in and shut the door quietly. He moved over to the passenger seat to see that his dad was done filling the tank and had closed the lid. Victor turned the car key and started the car, driving right out of there. At that moment, Natalie and Susan came out and Susan asked, "What's going on? Where's he going?!"

David yelled, "I don't know! Victor!"

"Victor, stop!" yelled Susan.

They helplessly watched Victor drive away, confused and petrified, forced to discuss what they should do next. David walked straight into the store, planning on calling the sheriff and telling him to return his son and car.

Victor kept his eyes on the road. Sometimes he found himself taking his foot off the gas and the car would almost stop as he was trying to get used to the steering as much as the speed. The main thing he had to be careful of was to not get pulled over. But no matter what circumstances, he would keep driving to get back before night would come.

Chapter Seven

Concerned Victor would hurt or kill himself, David went inside to call the police to stop him. They felt helpless knowing they couldn't do anything. David approached Susan and asked, "Did you know anything about this?"

"No, believe me, I'm just as shocked as you are."

David looked at Natalie to ask her as well. "What about you? Did you know this was going to happen?"

Natalie was nervous and was looking down until she rolled them back up to answer, "No."

David asked again, "Natalie, tell us the truth. It's imperative that you do."

"I said I didn't."

"Be honest, did you take part in this?"

"Look, why do you even have to nag me on this anyway? Since when do I ever hide anything for

Victor? And besides, maybe he was right in what he said about me back in the shop. I pretend to know him but I don't and I've always been a bitch for always calling him out."

"Let's not fall from the subject here because I'm still asking you to be honest. DID YOU KNOW ABOUT THIS?!"

Natalie was afraid to see her parents' anger when she said, "Alright look, Victor told me not to tell but now that he's gone I might as well. Before we left he told me that once we reached this gas station he was going to take the car back into town to meet up with Steven and kill those things. I'm really sorry I kept this from you and I probably shouldn't have."

David was very angry at this point, "No, you shouldn't have!"

"Hush, David, people are looking," said Susan.

David went on, "That's why you have to tell me these things so that none of you get hurt! You kids keep secrets these days and don't tell your parents anything. This is exactly why I ride you about these things more than usual, because you have always lied to us about everything."

Natalie didn't speak as she felt too embarrassed to

do so. Susan walked in front of David and asked, "Why did we even have to move here? Our life was perfect enough back in Seattle, so I blame some of this on you."

"Susan, please. No one could have predicted something like this."

"But still, why did we have to leave? Was it for us or for you? I just wish I was strong enough to tell you how I felt, but now it's too late."

David just turned his back on both of them and walked into the store to clear his head. Natalie was feeling really heavy as she couldn't figure out if this was the best decision she had ever made or the worst.

With Victor still driving back, he didn't know if his dad had called the cops and if they were waiting for him in town, although he did suspect it. Victor himself wanted to be a cop, ever since he saw Batman and how he fought to end crime, he thought why not a job where you can have a positive impact on society? After driving a few moments longer, he passed a sign that said, "Welcome to Roarke". He had already driven past the lake. Victor was starting to have second thoughts about going to the house and killing the werewolves, expecting they were still hiding in the shadows of their basement. Victor couldn't go without Steven since the two of them basically made a vow. Victor was worried about meeting Steven a little late, since he was driving for the first time. Fortunately he hadn't said he would meet Steven at 6:00 sharp, so being a few minutes late shouldn't be a problem. Victor wasn't even in the mood to listen to music like he always did while sitting in the passenger seat when his mom was driving. Now loud noises would only make him feel even more nervous.

Victor was tired from not getting enough sleep the night before, but luckily he managed to get to nap for a bit on the road to the gas station with his family. He even had a dream, a dream where he was at his house the night the werewolves attacked him and his family. Except this time he did not go to the house that belonged to the wolves. Instead, he stayed home the whole day after Willy told him not to go to the other side of the lake. Everyone was sitting at the kitchen table, and Victor stood up to walk away. When he turned back around and looked at his family, before he could say more than a few words, his family became motionless, staring and frightened of what appeared out of the darkness behind Victor. He looked at his sister, then his mom and dad, whose coffee cups were shaking in fear. He asked, "What... what are you looking at?"

He suddenly saw a hairy, humanlike hand with claws on his left shoulder, then it vanished when he woke up with a jerk. At first he didn't know what the dream meant, but he took it as a sign that Victor and his family would have died that night if Victor hadn't gone against what Willy told him that day and investigated.

Moments later he arrived back in town where a police officer was waiting for him. The commander had told him to look out for a grey van with an attached carrier behind it. When Victor drove by, the officer came out of hiding where he was waiting for Victor to enter town. The cop turned on his sirens, pulling in behind Victor. Victor wondered if the siren was for him then heard over the loudspeaker, "Victor Hyde, pull over."

Victor stepped on the gas to go faster. When they came to an intersection, Victor quickly moved before the light turned red. As for the cop, he was forced to stop to avoid hitting another car. Victor turned left into the mall parking lot and made a run for it. The cop pulled in quickly behind him, then jumped out to chase after him on foot. While chasing him, the cop spoke into the radio on his shoulder, "Sir, I've found Victor Hyde! He's running around the mall and I'm in pursuit!"

When Victor made his way around the mall, he saw another cop car coming. Victor ran across the street, into an alley. The other cop got out and began chasing him as well. Victor took a left once he reached the end of the alley, just down the street from where he was going to meet Steven. Steven was leaning with one foot against the wall, arms crossed, waiting for Victor. He looked over and saw Victor running toward him. Steven asked, "Victor, what's wrong? Why are you running?"

"They're chasing me, no time to explain. Run!

They came to another alley, which they ran down. Steven stopped Victor and pointed to a loading dock. The door was left open so they jumped in and closed the blinds, waiting for the cops to pass. They could hear them outside saying, "Where did they go?"

"I don't know but let's keep moving."

They waited a bit longer to be sure the police weren't there and Steven asked, "So, why were they chasing you?"

"Well, I believe my parents called them to be on the lookout for me when I came back to town. I stuck to the plan and didn't tell my parents about our plan. I took the car from that gas station you told me about just outside of town."

A man holding a crate came onto the loading dock and asked angrily, "What are you kids doing in here?"

Victor said, "Sorry sir, we're just hiding."

"Hiding from what?"

"Our friends, I guess you can say we're playing hide and seek. What's in these boxes?"

"Ice cream, and aren't you too old to be playing those games?"

"Of course not. I mean I can imagine someone your age playing it. My cousin would play it, only with their cars, where the person who's it would drive around to find the others in their cars driving around town."

"Well, go play somewhere else."

Victor said, "Okay sir, sorry about this."

Victor and Steven opened the door and after they left, the man shut the door behind them. "You know you were late, right?" asked Steven.

"Yeah well, I didn't expect company. Let's just get to your house and get supplies."

"Alright, I have to eat anyway."

They started walking to Steven's house to hide and

wait until it was time to move out. "So, I guess it wasn't easy?" asked Steven.

"What wasn't?"

"You disobeying your parents and having the will to outrun the cops, just so you could find more trouble later."

"I'm just doing what I need to, Steven. And like I said, you don't have to be a part of this."

"But I already am; and besides, I need to."

"What do you mean by that?" asked Victor.

"Never mind, let's just get to the house."

Soon they came to Steven's house and he introduced Victor to his mom. "Hi Mom, I'd like you to meet my friend. This is Victor. Victor, this is my mom, Tracy."

Victor said, "Hi," but also said, "Sorry if it's short notice but my parents are out of town and I have nowhere else to stay, so I asked Steven if I could stay the night."

"Hmm, sure, alright. When will your parents be back?"

"Hopefully tomorrow."

"And where have you been all day, Steven?"

"I've been at the arcade with him."

"Next time just be sure to let me know where you are."

"Okay, now can we please eat?"

"Sure. Victor would you like to join us?"

"No thanks, miss. I already had dinner, I'll be fine."

Steven said, "You can go upstairs if you want. Just don't steal anything. Ha! Ha!"

"Ha! Yeah, that's funny, Steven."

Victor walked upstairs to find Steven's room. He saw posters hanging on the wall and ceiling, and pictures of him that looked like he was trying to build a pyramid of cards when he was younger. Victor snooped into his drawers and found a collection of old newspaper articles. All of them involved disappearances. Victor even found a photo of Steven's dad in one of the articles that said, "Vet and Journalist Vanish."

Steven's dad was the veterinarian, and being a local in 1979, a photo journalist came to find out about the disappearances, hoping to get into National Geographic if the case was solved. Unfortunately, the two were not heard from the next day so Tracy panicked and insisted that the police search for him. The journalist seemed to have escaped the lake but in his motel room they found a pool of blood with dismembered body parts, most of which were not at the crime scene. Steven's dad's body was never recovered, so they presumed he was dead. After reading the article, Victor could understand why it meant so much to Steven to not stay behind. Steven came in within the next few minutes and asked, "Well, how do you like my room, Victor?"

"It's great and I like your posters on the wall. They're really neat. Your room is bigger than mine.

"Thanks, I knew you would like it."

"Steven, can I ask you something?"

"Yeah sure, I don't see why not."

"This thing you have of wanting to go to the lake, not just because you got involved in it last night but for revenge?"

"Revenge?"

Steven looked past Victor at his opened drawer with the articles out and said, "Oh you mean…"

"Your dad."

Steven gave Victor a positive nod with a deep sigh and said, "Yeah, my dad. I was seven when I lost him. Unlike my mom, he didn't fear the lake. I hated him for getting himself killed and me having to grow up without him. What has your Dad been like growing up?"

"My dad is a good man and I couldn't imagine anyone else being my father."

"Your dad sounds like an angel. I just wish I could've gotten to know him more in case I die tonight."

"You know Steven, there is always someone who is like an angel on your shoulder. Someone who is there when you need them and who becomes your most trusted partner-in-crime, to overcome the risks that life throws your way. It can be anyone; a parent, sibling, cousin, aunt, uncle, grandparent… a friend."

Steven looked at Victor and asked, "So, what you're saying is that you're supposed to be my guardian angel?"

"Ha, well I did save your life last night, didn't I?"

"Ha! Ha! That's true."

They looked at each other with a grin and knew from there on that they were friends. So they grabbed what they needed and before they made their way out the door Steven said, "Mom, we're just going out for a little while."

"To where?"

"To the arcade again."

"Okay, just don't stay out too late."

As they made their way out the door Victor asked, "So, do you have everything we need in that bag?"

"Yes, I have silver knives, a gun from my dad's safe, and garlic."

Victor looked inside to make sure and asked, "Why would you bring garlic? They're werewolves not vampires!"

"I know, but what if they're the same?"

Victor laughed to himself and Steven asked, "Why do we have to bring duct-tape?"

"So we can tie the knives around sticks once we get there. It's best to keep some distance between us and them. I even brought my camera."

"Why?"

"Well, noticing that these things don't like the light, it might be a good way to keep them away from us if we find ourselves in trouble."

The time was now around 7:00 p.m. and in a couple more hours, the sun would be down. The two had to hurry if they wanted to beat the werewolves at their game. Victor and Steven came to the mall where he left the car, got in and drove to the lake. But someone was watching them, a witness to the pursuit that occurred between Victor and the cop. She was an employee working at the supermarket next door to the mall and as soon as she saw Victor, she called the cops to tell them that he was there. When they got the call, an officer in the area heard on his radio that the suspect was now en route. The officer headed out in pursuit.

Victor was now heading out on the road out of town toward the lake. The cop was unsure where he had gone until he received word another eyewitness had seen someone just outside of town pulling a carrier on the back of the car. He stopped to speak to the witness while she was walking down the sidewalk.

He then rushed down the road to catch up with Victor. The officer radioed in to the sheriff, "Sir, that boy Victor, I'm following him up to where he's heading out of town and I'll call you when I bring him back in."

"I hear you. I believe he's going to the lake. I just got a call from his parents, they believe that's where he's going," said the sheriff. The officer was hesitant to chase him down through those woods at night but still pursued him.

"Great, we're facing werewolves. What's next, a gargoyle?" asked Steven.

"I know, right? Who would have ever known that monsters exist," said Victor with a humorous voice, then thought to himself and said, "Well, I guess there is one who knew the answer to that... Willy."

"When was the last time you saw him?"

"Last night when I ran. After he warned me about those wolves I ran back to the house and took my mom into town. Since then I haven't heard from him, but how could I since he's a man who totally keeps to himself. I just hope he's alright."

"I don't even know why you care so much about him. He's a bad guy."

"How can you say that?" asked Victor indignantly.

"He knew this whole time that those things existed and he didn't do anything about it, and because of that people are dead, including my father. I'm surprised that he's even still alive after living there for all those years. But personally if he is still alive, I'm going kill him myself."

"You'll do no such thing."

"Why not?"

"Look, I don't know much about Willy but you are right about him being wrong for keeping this from everyone all this time, for all the loved ones people lost. I'll give you that but you're not right for wanting to take his life away."

"Yeah well, I just hope he suffers," said Steven coldly.

"I can't possibly know how you feel since this never happened to me but I assure you, you can only hope for good things since hope should never be used for evil."

"I'm sorry, Victor. I just lost my temper."

"It's okay."

"I guess Willy is a good man. I wouldn't believe it if he had told me, but I believe it since you said it."

They reached the lake and parked the car in front of Victor's house. The rest of the way they had to move on foot.

The police officer came up behind them, parked his car beside theirs, got out and tried tracking them down through the woods. He spoke into his radio to tell his boss, "Sir, I've found the car. He parked it in front of his house but there is no one inside the car or his house. I'm going to investigate further, to find him in the woods. Over."

"Roger that, officer. Be sure to call in if you've found him and be on the lookout for any campers. I heard that five men decided to go out there tonight and I suppose they don't know that the lake is closed and condemned, so you should find them and force them to leave. Over and out."

Victor and Steven came upon Willy's shack. Victor checked to see if Willy was there but he was nowhere to be seen. Although he wanted to look further inside, they continued on their path, not wanting to waste time.

"So, do you know where this house is?" Steven asked.

"I hope so, we just have to keep following the path down to the lake and we'll probably find it."

"Probably?"

Victor looked at him with annoyance, "Well, I'm sure it's a lot better than should."

"Yes, definitely so."

"Dark clouds tonight."

"How can you tell?"

"You can't see any stars."

"Maybe there's a storm coming. I tell you, the one thing dogs have in common is that they're all afraid of thunder. Much like fireworks. My dog would always be out of sight whenever stuff like that would happen. Even when we would call him he wouldn't show."

"What kind of dog do you have?" asked Victor.

"A Jack Russell. She's seven years old and wouldn't stop crying on the first day, but I think it's like that for all dogs."

"I had a dog once. She was one of those Chinese ones with the mane around her neck."

"A Chow-Chow?" asked Steven.

"Yes."

"What was her name?"

"Cassie."

"She died when I was really young but I remember I would chase her around the house at night. I don't know how she would've taken to thunder."

"Yeah my dog, she would always hide under the bed when she would hear those louds booms in the sky."

"Yeah, it does look like rain…"

Chapter Eight

The night was far from over so until the next light, the five men set up camp. Their names were Jack, Bill, Raymond, Ben and Dylan. The entire day they spent fishing and cruising at the lake, not knowing they were just three hundred yards away from the Mallard house. Soon they would see if Victor or the werewolves would come upon them first.

Jack said to Dylan, "You sure caught a lot of fish."

"Yes, but isn't it illegal to catch six fish?"

"Ah!!! Who cares? No one comes here anyway!"

Ray asked, "Why is that? I mean, I've been living here for three years now and I still don't know why no one comes here."

"It's nothing. Just a local boogeyman story about people who come to this lake and are never seen again," said Jack.

Ray asked, "So, you all have been living here your whole lives and you're not scared at all?"

Ben said, "Well, I only believe something if I see it, and police always say no bodies were ever recovered. So in my opinion no one has been hurt or found dead."

Raymond was a little scared, but felt safe enough since he was with the others and they all had guns. He went on, "But what is the cause for this urban legend?"

Dylan responded, "Nobody knows."

"It certainly is a mystery," said Jack.

"Is that why you all brought guns?" asked Raymond.

Jack laughed, "Ha! No, I brought mine so I could shoot quail."

"Quail?" asked Ben.

"Yes, back in the sixties my uncle killed one in this area. At the time they were overpopulated in this territory, but I haven't seen one."

Raymond asked, "So wait, your uncle came here and left with a quail, he claimed?"

"Yes."

"I thought you said anyone who comes here is never seen again."

"Well it doesn't happen all the time. Only at night."

Ray stared with a stunned silence and a motionless body until Ben shouted, "Boo!"

Ray jumped, looking at Ben all frustrated and slowing his breath. They all laughed seeing Ray scared. Jack said, "I guess you do believe that story to be true."

"What's not to believe?" said Bill.

"What are you talking about, Bill?" asked Jack.

"Well, there is something about this lake most people don't know and that is people disappear because they are mauled by a pack of animals."

"By what... wolves?" asked Ben.

"Getting warmer. Wolves, yes; humans, yes."

Jack asked, "What are you saying? You don't believe that... impossible. There's no way. Where would you even pick this up?"

"Just something about there once being four brothers whose father was the founder of this town in the early eighteen hundreds. Then they were never seen again, or at least no one's lived to tell about it."

"So how do they become werewolves, how does that come in?"

"Some curse put on them. I don't know, I can't remember."

"But who told you this?" asked Ben.

"An old war vet that lives on this lake."

"What's his name?"

"Willy."

Jack said, "Hmm, interesting, a hermit who lives alone and avoids human society. Sounds like a twisted guy to me."

"Well, I don't believe he's the killer if that's what you're saying," said Bill.

"Well, if that were true, if I even thought that story was true I'm sure I wouldn't be here right now," said Ben arrogantly.

"You know you're right, Ben, so I guess you have nothing to worry about," said Bill sarcastically.

After their conversation, they started cooking the fish they caught that day. Dylan and Raymond gutted the fish and got rid of their organs by throwing them in the bushes. It was a disgusting way because usually people would put them in plastic bags and later throw them in the garbage. They sterilized the fish by roasting them over the fire to kill any bacteria.

It was now completely dark and Ray was staying close to the fire after that frightening story. As for the wolves, they were now coming out of their house to go on the hunt for Victor again, but picked up the scent that someone else was there. Once they moved two hundred yards through the forest, they lifted their heads from the ground and saw a glow of light past the trees. The wolves circled around their campsite to see how many there were and any weaknesses around the camp.

Bill, Jack and Dylan went into the woods with their guns and left Ben and Raymond at the campsite. Dylan asked, "So why are we hunting in the dark?"

"Who said anything about hunting?" said Bill.

"Are we going back to the truck for something?"

"No."

"Well then, you mind telling me what we're doing out here?" asked Dylan beseechingly.

"Nothing, just taking a walk in the woods with my friends."

"Well, what about Ray and Ben, they're your friends."

"I've only met Ray four times and Ben... well, you know how it works between me and him. It was never my idea to bring either of them here, and personally I don't care much for either of them."

Both Jack and Dylan were beginning to feel apprehensive about how Bill felt for the other two, especially Ben. They knew Ben was never the friendliest to Bill in or outside of work, but they had still been friends since they were kids. Bill once told Dylan that the two were no longer friends, just two totally different people. So true, it was not Bill's idea to bring Ben or Ray out here, but to Dylan there seemed to have been something else going through Bill's mind and it didn't seem like it was going to be pleasant.

Back at the campsite Ben and Ray started talking

about the other guys. "So, how come we couldn't go with them?" asked Ray.

"I don't know, but someone has to stay by the campfire anyway."

"Well, I like the idea of staying close to the fire. I don't want to be out in those woods."

"But we already are," said Ben.

"Ah yeah, right."

"Don't tell me you're afraid, that you actually believe Bill's story."

"No... of c-c-c-course not," said Ray stuttering.

"Your stuttering is very reassuring."

"May I ask though, why does he hate you?"

"Who?"

"Bill. I've seen the way he looks at you when he talks to you."

"Bill and I have been friends since before we met Jack and Dylan in high school, but after graduation we drifted apart. We kinda came back together by working at the same company. Unfortunately it wasn't enough as it became worse than when we were kids."

Soon after, Ray could hear sounds from behind him. Both Ray and Ben got up, one after the other, and Ben asked, "What is it?"

"I heard something."

"Heard what?"

"I don't know."

Ray moved toward a bush with his rifle and slowly pointed it into the bush. One of the werewolves who was crouched in the bush grabbed the end of the gun. Ray tried to pull it back but the wolf easily pulled it right out of his hands. Ray, shocked, just stood there, and before he could even inhale, the wolf leaped out from the bush and on top of him, hitting the ground hard. Ben shouted "Oh fuck!!!" and started to flee for his life.

Ray struggled, trying desperately to get the wolf off him, but took a claw mark to the face. Ray shouted, "No! Stop! No!" He took a bite to the neck and began to choke, bleeding to death. The werewolf stood up, stomping three times, crushing Ray's face.

Bill, Jack and Dylan came to what seemed to be a

cave. Jack wanted to take a further look. Dylan warned him by saying, "Careful Jack, there could be a bear in there."

Jack led the way in with his flashlight, being the only one who took one from camp. Inside the cave, there seemed to have been nothing living in it for a while, but on the walls they saw what appeared to be Native American wall paintings. They couldn't understand them but they could tell which ones were humans and which were animals. The animals they saw on the wall looked like werewolves. A human-shaped wolf creature that natives once feared and even worshipped before they were killed. Even with these signs, they still did not believe, but the look on Bill's face meant that he knew it was more than just a legend. They walked out of the cave and decided to head back to camp.

On their way back, Dylan walked close to Jack, who was behind Bill. "Jack, those wall paintings were real, right?"

"How do you mean, real?"

"Well, do you think they told an actual story?"

"You mean about the werewolves?"

"Yes, of course."

"Look, there's no such thing as werewolves. Legends like that are just made up to tell others scary stories around a campfire, like today. Ha!"

After Ben deserted the campsite and his friend, he searched for some kind of trail that would lead him back to the road, knowing he may not be able to find the truck in the dark. He didn't want to stop, and hoped that a car would see him on the road to take him back into town. Down the narrow trail he ran until he heard a snarl from a distance behind him. He quickly looked behind with his eyes wide open and his heart beating rapidly, sweat trickling down the back of his neck. Ben backed away about six feet from where he was standing and stopped again. As he kept his gun raised, he heard something breathing to his right. He looked over, terrified, and could clearly see that the werewolf was there. He tried to point his gun toward him to shoot, but the werewolf lunged forward and took Ben down to the ground, identical to how they did to Ray. The werewolf bit off Ben's right hand when he tried to hit him, leaving Ben screaming in agonizing pain. The werewolf held him down with his left arm and used his right to plunge his way through Ben's chest and pulled out his heart. The werewolf rose above Ben, with the heart in his hand, watching it beat until it finally died out, just as Ben did. The werewolf ate Ben's heart then ran back to join his brother to attack the other three men.

As the three men were making their way back to camp, Jack found a bush of berries. He whispered, "You two go on, I want to collect these before I get back."

"Okay, just don't take long," said Dylan.

Arriving back at the camp and not seeing Ben or Ray, Dylan asked, "Where are they?"

"I don't know."

"Well, they couldn't have just left, could they?"

They looked around the camp, not finding anything until Bill found a small puddle of blood in the sand. He warily stated, "Well, I'm not certain where they are... but it looks like they were attacked by some animal."

"What?" screamed Dylan.

"Yeah, I'm not kidding, come take a look." Dylan walked over to see the blood and noticed the frightened look on Bill's face.

While Jack was still collecting berries, he heard a noise from the tree above him. He said to himself, "Huh, well I guess even squirrels would be good to roast over the fire."

He pointed his gun up in the air, looking for squirrels to shoot, then heard a loud thud on the ground, as if something fell out of the sky. He moved in to investigate, seeing a hole in the ground big enough to be a bear bed. He scanned around him, looking at the trees, then started to back away to where he first was. Before he could start back to camp, something else hit the ground, falling from the tree Jack was standing under. Right in front of him was a body. The face was too smashed to recognize but by looking at the clothes he could tell who it was and he shrieked, "Ray?"

"I've got to go tell..." he started but was cut off by a punch from behind that went clear through his chest. Barely breathing, he dropped the gun, triggering a gunshot that alerted Bill and Dylan.

"What was that?" asked Dylan.

"Sounds like Jack shot himself a buck."

Dylan looked at Bill with frustration and said, "Do you not care about this at all?"

"What do you mean?" asked Bill scornfully.

"Well, since this trip, even before it started, you've been a sour-puss. You've been distant from us, especially Ben, and now two people are missing. They could be hurt and you don't seem worried at all."

"Yeah well, if it makes you feel better, let's go back to find Jack."

"That's not what... oh, whatever."

The two walked through the woods to find Jack. Dylan tripped and fell to the ground. Before he got up he could smell something revolting. He couldn't see what it was since it was dark, even though it was right in front of him. As soon as his eyes adjusted he could see that it was Ray's deceased body. He stood up in front of Bill and shouted, "Bill, it's Ray! He's dead!"

Dylan looked down at the demolished face of Ray's body. He looked away from the sight of it, only to see another dead body near them. He walked over and crouched down to discover that it was Jack. "What could have done this to them?" asked Dylan, frightened.

"Like I said, just a wild animal," said Bill casually.

"Well, where is it?"

"How should I know?"

"Bill, we have to leave."

"What's the hurry?"

"What's the hurry?! After everything, how the fuck are you not scared? Now at least three men are dead, we're weak, and we've got a man-eater on our hands now. We need to leave and tell the sheriff about all of this immediately."

"Sure, I'll leave now, but not because of what you said but because what's done is done."

"What are you talking about?"

"The more you ask questions, the more you waste time keeping us here with your paranoia."

They walked away, on their way back to the truck. Dylan was really confused, scared and angry about what was going on. He especially couldn't fathom how Bill still had that same poker face after everything that had happened tonight. Bill was just behaving like nothing was wrong, almost like he planned for something like this to happen.

Before the group left that day, Dylan had told his mom, sick in bed, that he would stay with her and pass on going with his friends to the lake, but his mom insisted that he go. He needed time for himself and he earned it after looking out for her every single day. He'd even passed on going on a date with a lovely girl named Alice, upset when she started dating Jack after he had turned her down. But out of all the men in the world, why Jack, he thought to himself. Was it to make him jealous or because she really did care about him? Though she hardly knew Jack, the moment she saw him talking to Dylan and found out they were friends, she started flirting with him. Dylan's mother felt bad when she found out that he had turned down such a pretty girl, all just for her, and grew tired of seeing him waste his days watching over her. She even told him that one day there would come a time when he would just have to let go.

He asked, "Like, let go of you?"

She said that because what mattered to her was for her son to be happy. even if that meant without her. She knew that she wasn't always going to be around. His mother wanted him to live out his life with a family of his own, and it wasn't worth losing that chance for her sake.

But to Dylan it would break his heart, and he only trusted himself to watch over her rather than hire someone else to be her nurse. For her though, he went camping because she wanted him to try to make it a fun event for himself.

Little did she know that it was the lake they were going to, as she herself had grown up knowing about the horrible tragedies that had happened at that lake. Since her sickness she had forgotten that part of her past since she didn't hear much about the outside world. She had been fighting this stomach cancer for years, even before her husband died. She didn't like goodbyes but knew she would see her son again. When he was leaving she gave him a kiss goodbye, and sometime after he left, she rested on her bed, and closed her eyes to rest in peace.

In the dark Dylan and Bill seemed lost. Dylan had a weird feeling. He couldn't describe it, but he felt that someone was watching them. He whispered, "So, how are we supposed to tell the sheriff what happened here tonight? Two of our friends are dead, and we don't know what happened to Ben."

"He's probably dead too," said Bill aloofly.

"How can you say that?"

"Why not? I mean, he's out there alone and probably got what's coming to him."

"Alright Bill, I get you hate Ben, Ray, Jack… and me but what about yourself?"

"Did I say I was good?"

"No, I mean, are you scared at all for your life?

Wait, what did you mean by that?"

"By what?"

"What you just said about yourself. Don't play dumb with me, Bill."

"Look Dylan, I don't care how long we've known each other. Even the oldest of friends can make the worst of enemies. The thing about us human beings is that we all deceive each other. Even friends tend to uprise against their own pals… And next time you speak behind someone's back, be sure to wait until after class."

"What are you talking about?"

"I remember hearing you in class when you were sitting right next to Jack. You looked over at me and were making fun of me to Jack about how much better you could have been if you weren't homeschooled by your parents. You continuously said I was inferior with anything to do with education. I can't believe my own friend would say such hurtful words about me, and in front of me, Dylan. I would have never said or treated you that way. Then again, we all still tend to do something we thought we would never do."

"So you're still pissed at me for something I did in

the past, is that it? Besides, things have changed since high school so I wouldn't do that to you anymore."

"Well you see now, Dylan, it's not about what you would do but what you could do. You, me, Jack, Ben and Ray. Everyone!"

"Yes, but you can't be cynical toward everyone. How would you expect to live?"

"Well, I guess the world would be a boring place if there wasn't some bad, but it doesn't mean everyone should have to be conceited. To hiss behind someone's back and try to make themselves look better than the other."

"You're right." Bill stopped and looked at Dylan, interested to hear what he had to say. He went on, "Look, let's just get back to the truck and tell the sheriff what happened here."

Dylan then turned his back to Bill and started walking. "Oh yeah sure, let's run along. Run back to your mother, mama's boy!" Bill muttered.

Dylan stopped with a fuming look on his face and turned to look back at Bill. "Well, look who's trying to cover himself up now."

"Yeah well, that's exactly what I've been talking

about this whole time. Anyone will try to put you on the spot. People have always done it to me, and for what? I can appreciate honesty, but not when someone comes off aggressive about it. I believe it is all about your approach, and I would appreciate it if people could keep their comments to themselves if it's something negative or useless to me. Getting it from my family is one thing, but a stranger or even your friend cannot presume to call anyone out for how you feel toward them at any given time."

"What's even worse is when people refuse to accept that they're wrong. I'll admit I'm not perfect, and sometimes try to cover up my mistakes with excuses. At least I can admit my wrongs."

"Look, I see you're really uptight about this and I respect your opinion about people, but let me ask you something. Why are you here? I mean, you made it pretty clear that you don't want any friends, so what are you doing here then?"

"Well, if you want to get into more detail, here's one. Two friends go camping. They've been friends longer than they can remember. They bring snacks with them, camping gear and tools. The irritating one says, 'So, it's too bad the others couldn't join us. I could've called up my cousin to come camping, but he was going out of town.' The other man says, 'Yeah, that is pretty bad.' Only he doesn't really care, but why not since he doesn't care about his friend as he once did. Four years back they met in Grade 11. They were both in musical theatre. The friend told him how good he was, but he begins to become even better. The friend grows jealous and tries to come up with any excuse to tell others he's bad, just to cover himself because he's scared of him being the center of attention. So when he hears him talking like this to him and later behind his back, that was when he crossed the line. The talented one just decided to avoid him the rest of the semester. The friend becomes concerned as to why his buddy no longer talks and looks at him anymore. Even whenever his friend was in the theatre he would go somewhere else, ultimately avoiding him. Finally the friend asks, 'Why do you hate me?' But the friend doesn't answer and gives him a look of disdain for saying things he would never say against his own friend."

"But of course, at the end of the semester when they put on their play, the friend forgave him but that didn't mean they were still friends since he never spoke to him until sometime after graduation, in their early twenties when he invited him to go camping. The next morning it would seem that the man was dismembered. Investigators examine the body and lock up the other friend as a possible suspect. He told them he was with them that night but didn't kill him. To prove his innocence they examine the body and determine it was mauled by a wild animal."

"Not only that but it turns out that for two months, the guy's girlfriend had been cheating on him with his old friend who hadn't really been his friend since high school. And if he didn't cross the line before, well he did now and was getting what was coming to him. So to even the score the friend invited him, pretending to be his friend again, when all he could think about was wanting him dead. For the whole day at the lake they have fun talking about their lives but he had it played out well, making the other guy believe that they were pals again."

"At night, the two have kabobs around the fire. One thought he had in his head was that after he was done eating he was going to take his kabob stick and plunge it through his eye. Of course, that would just make it too simple for the cops to find out it was murder. And if he dumped the body, people would immediately suspect him.

After the two go to sleep, the other one grabs himself a torch and puts out the campfire. He goes to take a stroll through the woods and leave the other guy behind. Within the hour, as he expected, a grizzly bear comes to the camp and sniffs around. Moving its nose across the tent, not knowing what to make of it, the bear walks into the tent after the friend left it unzipped before he left. On top of the other guy the bear sniffs and snarls in his face until the man wakes up and gasps in shock, moving under the bear, panicking. The bear starts clawing him up and biting his arm while the man tries fending him off. With no weapon beside him and the bear all over him, the man becomes powerless after the limb of his right arm was partially wrecked and torn off and his left ribs broken. Moving his left hand across the bear's face trying to stop it, the bear bites off three of his fingers. By the next morning the friend looks in the tent and sees the bloody mess the bear left behind. After that he calls the police and tells them his friend was killed. After a week, the case is closed due to lack of evidence that he killed him."

"Okay, so could I ask you one question?" asked Dylan.

"Sure, go ahead and shoot."

"Where did you pick up a story like that? I mean, how do you know it's true?"

"Did I say it was true… no. I'm just telling you what can happen when you're deceived by others or why people would want to do that to you."

"You're a murderer."

"No, no, they murdered them but unlike them, I'm still alive and I'm going to laugh when I see them kill you too."

"I'm going to tell the police what you've done!"

"You see, that's where you're wrong, Dylan."

"Go ahead, shoot. The police are going to match the shot with that gun."

"I'm not going to shoot you, but you won't get out of here alive, nor will anyone find you."

"Oh and I suppose you are, you're going to survive tonight?'

"Whether I do tonight or not, at least I got my revenge."

Dylan raised his gun and said, "Oh yeah, well you're not, because I'm going to."

Out of nowhere, Dylan is tackled to the ground and mauled by one of the wolves. Bill hears a growl near him and runs. Dylan shouts, "Help me!"

Not wanting to let Dylan die like this, Bill turned and shot Dylan with his rifle from forty yards to let him go quickly and painlessly. The second wolf came out of hiding and appeared to give its pack member a signal to leave the body and attack Bill. Bill continued running through the woods to get to the truck. He was lost and didn't know which way to go. He soon came to the same trail Ben was on, only to discover Ben's dead body. He ran up the trail, hoping to find a road but instead found an old fire tower. Rather than climbing up the tower only to have himself cornered, he continued on his way, alternating through the woods. He soon collapsed to the ground with grief, thinking about why he didn't want Dylan to die dreadfully, unlike the others, when he wasn't there to see it.

But now something else had changed. He no longer wanted to die, but instead wanted to make it out alive. Although he was even more scared to face the families of the deceased to tell them that it was his doing as to why the guys were dead, he got back on his feet. Before he could go any further, he heard heavy breathing to his right. He slowly turned to see a werewolf standing on two legs. Looking at it, he felt like he was looking at just another man that wanted to kill him. The posture of the wolf was so humanlike and it gave Bill a taunting look as he raised his gun to fire. With lightning speed, the wolf evaded the shot and disappeared into the woods. Bill turned to run again but standing above him was another one of the wolves. With its hand raised high in the air, it brought its arm down, striking Bill across the face with a powerful blow, leaving scratch marks across his cheeks. Bill was groveling on the ground until the second wolf walked up with its feet right in front of him. He looked up at it and yelled, "Fuck You!"

before they started mauling him, tearing his limbs off, killing him due to blood loss. As the wolves were about to dispose of all the bodies, they sensed something – it was the presence of another man.

Chapter Nine

It would seem that the odds were now more in favor of the werewolves than in Victor and Steven, who were coming to them.

Back at the gas station, Victor's dad got a call from the sheriff. He answered, "Hello."

"It's me, Sheriff Ramone."

"Have you found Victor yet?"

"Yes, but why did he run away from us when we tried to confront him?"

"He didn't want you to take him back to the station."

"Why is he trying to run away? And if he was running away, why did he come back into town? He must have known he'd get caught."

David was too embarrassed to tell him the truth, but knew the sheriff had to find his son. "Alright look, you're not going to believe me, but last night

Ollie's store was under attack and we tried keeping them out all night."

"What are you talking about, what attacked you?"

"It wasn't a man."

"Yeah, I get that. The doctor told me that the victim's wounds were from a wild animal. Was it a bear, mountain lion?"

"No…"

"Then what?"

"Werewolves, four of them. They came from the lake to kill my son and the rest of us. Victor managed to kill two of them but the others escaped."

"Mr. Hyde, I am trying to conduct a real police matter and I can't help you until you tell me the truth."

"I am! Look, there's nothing else I can tell you except that my son is in danger and he's risking it even more because he wants to return to the lake and kill those things."

"Are you certain that's where he's going?"

"Yes, why don't you believe me?"

"I'm only doing my job, which is to bring back your son, not to hunt down a children's story. I'll talk to you later, if anything else happens."

"Just please make sure my son does not die."

"I'll speak to you later."

After hanging up, David felt helpless, not being able to do anything but wait. Even the sheriff didn't sound too convincing about bringing Victor back alive, but probably only because the sheriff doubted that Victor was in trouble because of werewolves.

Back at the lake, Victor and Steven came upon one of the bodies. It was Bill, who was dismembered, then soon Dylan. Victor recognized them and said, "I know these guys. I saw them in town earlier today."

"Did you speak to them?" asked Steven.

"No, but there were five of them and they mentioned going camping at the lake."

"Okay then, where's the rest of their party?"

"I don't know but this means the werewolves were

just here and they're not too far away. We should hurry."

"Right behind you."

They started walking and within 100 yards they came to the manor. The stench was just as Victor remembered it. There was no sign of the wolves.

The sheriff and his deputies reached the lake, planning to make their way down the water to find Victor, to help the deputy that had arrived previously and was already looking for Victor and Steven.

"So, where are they?" asked Steven.

"I don't know but stay close. I figure those other guys didn't have the same idea. Keep your back toward mine. That way we have eyes all around us."

"Good idea!" said Steven.

Outside the house, in front of the basement window, was a body that wasn't moving. When Victor got close, with Steven right behind him, he reached out to turn over the body to see their face... it was Willy. Willy was really torn up and Victor's heart was so heavy that he wanted to cry.

Steven asked, "Is that Willy?"

"Yes it is."

They looked at Willy, feeling sorry for him, seeing how gruesomely he had been clawed and bitten to death. Beside Willy, in the leaves, they found wire strung around the walls of the house. Victor looked around and saw one of the wires led back to a box, while the others were attached to dynamite. Victor realized what Willy had been trying to do. Suddenly, one of the wolves made a loud howl and charged down the stairs to attack.

The sheriff and his men heard the howl and one said, "Huh? Wolves? I don't think there's been a sighting in this town for over forty years."

Another deputy said, "Yeah well, if we do find one tonight, I'm going to kill it."

"Quiet! We have to hurry," said the sheriff.

The deputies were puzzled, while the sheriff was driven to follow the howls and got them to start moving again.

One of the wolves jumped out of the downstairs window. Victor shot at it, but missed. The wolf zig-zagged its way away from Victor and Steven. The two moved in circles, back to back. Victor only had four bullets left in his gun. He also had his camera around his neck so he would be able to take pictures of the wolves as proof for the police.

The wolf came out from behind a bush, taunting Victor. Victor raised the gun but the wolf, using its incredibly fast reflexes, dodged the bullets as Victor shot at it twice. The wolf leaped at them. Victor yelled, "Duck!"

The second werewolf came out from the trees to join the fight but the wolves felt the presence of someone else coming, so they retreated into the forest.

"Why did they run away?" asked Steven.

"I don't know."

The sheriff's deputy who was sent to pursue Victor and Steven burst out of the trees. The deputy and Victor pointed guns at each other before they spoke. "Who are you?" asked Victor.

"I'm Deputy Maier, I was sent here to find you."

"Yeah well, we can't go back yet. We have something here we need to finish."

"What's that?"

"I can't tell you but we need your help."

"Okay... sure, but I need you to put your gun down first."

"Do it, Victor," said Steven. "Victor, come on, he's a cop!"

"If I give him my gun, then the wolves will kill us both."

"Just trust him. I don't want either of us to get shot."

Victor slowly lowered his gun to the ground after being calmed by Steven's words. The deputy asked them to step back while he walked over to pick up the gun saying, "Okay, now tell me what's really going on."

"My friend and I came here to put down two dangerous animals that have been killing others."

"What kind? Bear, mountain lion... wolves?"

"Wolves!" said Steven.

"So where are they now?"

"They were just here until you fucking showed

up!" Victor shouted.

"Hey… watch it, especially how you talk to an officer of the law. Now let's go."

"Whoa! Wait, what about the wolves?" asked Steven.

"Myself and the rest of the deputies will handle it later. Right now it's my job to bring the both of you back to your parents."

"I already told you we can't leave yet," said Victor.

"Look, I don't know what it is that makes you guys want to risk your lives for something that police can handle, or why you would even give a shit after that stunt you pulled today."

Victor snickered, "Something that the police can handle. You know, I can't believe how blind this town is. This whole killing spree has been going on since before President Andrew Jackson, and you want to tell me it's all under control."

"What are you talking about?" asked the deputy.

"Never mind. If someone else dies it's on your hands. Look, bottom line is, I can't leave. If I do they'll just come after me."

The deputy stopped Victor from talking and tried to forcefully take him away but Victor hit him. The deputy let go of his arm as he fell to the ground. "Alright kid, when we get to town, I'm taking you to jail. I'd say up to thirty days for a punishable offence will be about right."

"For what?" asked Victor.

"For hijacking a car, carrying an unlicensed weapon, and assaulting an officer of the law."

"Oh c'mon!"

"Yes! Underage or not, I'm putting these handcuffs on you."

Suddenly a snarl from the trees stopped the deputy. "What was that?" asked the deputy.

"It's them!" said Steven.

"You mean the wolves?"

"Yes, they're stalking us."

"Yeah well, that's what wolves do before they attack. Now let's get moving."

"We can't now. We're here and our only chance

now is to kill them before they kill us."

"C'mon, it's not like they can jump from the sky."

The deputy said that just before one of the wolves jumped from a tree above them, killing him on impact. With the werewolf on top of him, Victor and Steven couldn't get to the guns without getting hurt. Steven kept his spear in front of him to keep the werewolf away, while Victor quickly thought of a plan. He whispered, "Steven, you stay outside, I'm going to lure them into the house."

"What?!"

"You see that box over there? When I lure them in, you run over and get ready to blast the thing. When I say 'now', blow it."

"But…"

"Just do it!"

Victor ran over and saw the second wolf come out from the woods. He started throwing rocks at the glass windows yelling, "Hey, over here! Come and get me!"

Enraged, the wolves ran after him and away from Steven. Steven did what Victor said and ran over to the box to get ready to push the lever.

Down the main hallway Victor ran, seeing the wolves run in through the front door. The first wolf charged down the hall, knocking down the grandfather clock, and leapt at Victor. Victor darted out of the way and ran into the living room.

The wolf that leapt at Victor and missed went clear through the wall of the house, to the outside. Victor quickly made his way from the living room to the dining room. When he reached the front door, he was blocked by the second wolf. Feeling trapped, staring at it and not knowing what to do, he quickly got closer and took a picture of it, the flash blinding it. While it was struggling, Victor ran out the front door and shouted, "Now!"

Steven immediately pressed down on the lever, causing the dynamite to blow and the house to collapse.

Steven rose up saying, "That was for my dad!"

Victor walked over to Steven and the two of them looked at the ruined house with Steven asking, "So, do you think they're dead?"

"I hope so." Victor gave him a head nod and said, "Let's find out."

They walked over, stepping over the huge wood pile that they began to search through.

The sheriff and his deputies heard the explosion and one of them asked, "What was that loud boom we heard? That sure was no gunshot."

Another deputy said, "Sounded like an explosion, but from what?"

"We heard gunshots not too long ago. You think they were from Maier?"

"How should I know?"

"Well sorry for asking!"

"Why did you say that?"

"Say what?"

"Sorry for asking."

"I don't know, you just don't seem to be in the best mood."

"C'mon, I just said how should I know."

"It's how you said it."

"You have to be that sensitive on the job?"

"Will you two quit your bullshit!" yelled the sheriff.

Back at the house Victor and Steven were having trouble digging through the debris. Soon they found the first wolf who had turned back into its human form after death.

The other wolf survived and was watching them from the trees, planning its next move. At this point the wolf feared Victor, unlike anyone it had before, but was still not going to leave until it finished what was started. Thoughts of what the wolf should do surged through its mind, working through what he was going to do after he killed Victor and Steven, and where he would go afterward.

Fortunately, Victor and Steven were some of the few that had actually seen the wolves, and if it killed them, no one else would know. Even if someone said something, who would believe them?

The wolf didn't know that Victor knew it was watching them from the trees. Victor kept digging, just as Steven did, to make himself look unaware of the wolf's presence. Like they did to the deputy, the wolf climbed up the tree to attack from high ground so they wouldn't see it coming. Victor didn't let down his guard though because he knew what the werewolf wanted.

Victor realized the wolf was waiting for him to look away, so he slowly turned his back from the tree, then turned back quickly. At that moment, as expected, the werewolf jumped from the tree to attack Victor, but Victor moved swiftly out of the way. Victor ran to grab Steven's spear while Steven grabbed a 2x4 from the debris to use as a blunt object. With the spear pointed toward the wolf, the wolf gave Victor a ferocious look, thinking of the vendetta he had against Victor for killing the others.

Steven ran over to attack the wolf with the piece of wood, but the wolf looked back at Steven. As Steven went in for the swing, the wolf grabbed him. As he was going in for a bite, Steven swung his wrist and forearm, using the piece of wood to gag the werewolf, stopping the crushing bite.

The wolf heard Victor running toward him with his spear, ready to attack, so he quickly threw Steven about thirteen feet away to clear the space between him and Victor. As Victor jabbed his spear at the wolf's head, it grabbed it with its mouth, biting off the knife at the end of the spear. Victor tried using what was left of the spear, swinging it at the werewolf, but it grabbed the end, lifting it up with Victor holding on. He lifted Victor off his feet, tossing and slamming him to the ground. Victor saw the knife on the ground, grabbed it to fight again, right as the police arrived.

When the sheriff and his six deputies arrived, they saw the deceased Maier, the huge pile of debris, along with the werewolf, shocking them all as they pulled out their guns. The wolf tried to retreat as Victor shouted, "Not this time!"

Victor jumped on the wolf, knife in hand. The wolf struggled, trying to throw Victor off, but he held on. Victor gripped his left arm around the wolf, plunging the knife into its heart with his right. The werewolf started howling and shaking Victor off, then dropped to its knees, holding one hand on its heart while the other was on the ground. The werewolf turned to look at the cops, Steven, then Victor, right before it fell to the ground. As it hit the ground, they watched as it changed from its werewolf body to its human-form right before their eyes. They could now see the corpse of the eldest son, James Mallard.

Victor walked up to Steven and asked, "Are you okay?"

"I'll be alright. You?"

"I am now."

The sheriff walked up to them and said, "Well… I guess if I'm not crazy then your family isn't either. I'll have deputies clean this up and I'll take you both back to your parents."

"We'd be grateful for that, sheriff," replied Victor.

The three of them made their way down the lake to the sheriff's car. He first took Victor back to see his family who were waiting for him back in town, then took Steven back to his mother.

Victor's family was waiting for him at the police station. He was extremely nervous to face them after risking his life like that, but once they saw him get out of the car, they couldn't stop hugging him. Victor was surprised that none of them yelled in his face but gratefully hugged them back, happy to be with his family again. Soon they got into their car, which had been brought there earlier from the supermarket where Victor had left it. They were going to be staying in a motel for the night.

Once they arrived at the motel, they unpacked and got settled in. No one bothered to ask Victor any questions about what happened but their silence seemed very reassuring to each of them.

Victor told them about Willy and what he had tried to do. Victor pleaded with his parents to arrange a funeral for Willy. David told Victor that they would most certainly arrange it. Shortly after, Victor walked outside and looked out through the night and at the moon as he heard a loud howl of a wolf, knowing in his heart that it was just the howl of a natural grey wolf. He knew the threat was finally over.

Chapter Ten

Victor and his family decided that after the funeral passed, they would not leave town. Victor didn't go back to school for a week, giving the family time to find a way to get back to reality after everything that had happened to them.

One week later, Victor's father had Willy's funeral arranged and it was finally going to happen this afternoon. Before school Victor had a talk with his mother, "Mom, are you coming to the funeral today?"

"Of course," said Susan feeling hurt. "How could you ask me that?"

"Sorry, Mom. I know I shouldn't ask my own mother something like that."

"No, I'm sorry, Victor. I think I can see why you would ask. I feel awful. I wish I hadn't been so cruel to him and now he's dead."

"Mom, don't worry, I made sure that he didn't die in vain. He tried to do us a favor; now we must do him one."

"I love you, Victor. I am so proud of you and I know your father is too."

"I love you too, Mom."

When they were finished eating breakfast, Victor's mom took him to school. It was Friday and they were looking forward to having the weekend off. When Susan dropped Victor off, it seemed like a new welcoming, much better than the first day Victor arrived at the school.

Steven, Ham, Keller, Danny and Fuller – the whole gang was there. The first one to say hi was Ham when he said, "Hey Victor, how are you doing?"

"Oh great! Hey, Steven."

"Hey, Victor."

"Hey Victor, I have some people here I'd like to introduce you to," said Ham. "This is Danny, you've seen him at Ollie's. This is Keller, as you know, from Photo Class, and this is Fuller."

"Nice to meet you all. So you want to head inside?"

"Sure, let's go."

They walked into the school together with Victor asking Ham, "So Ham, what gives with you hanging out with these guys?"

"What do you mean?"

"Well, no offence or anything, it's just I thought you didn't like Danny or Keller. Well, I know that you're friends with Danny but I hear you guys are actually frenemies?"

"Yes true, but for the last week I've gotten to become friends with Keller. We've been hanging out a lot after school and going to Ollie's. As for Danny, yes he can be quite the prankster but he usually means well."

As they walked down the hall together, everyone kept gawking at Victor. "Why is everyone staring at us?" asked Victor.

"Not us, you," said Ham.

"Well, that's weird."

"What's weird? People have been talking; they know about that hot pursuit between you and the cops."

"Really, do they know anything else?"

"They know about the incident at Ollie's and about the funeral."

"Yes, that's all true but they still don't know anything about the depth of the story."

They soon came to their lockers. Danny and Fuller headed off together to their classes while Steven and Keller stayed to chat before the first bell rang. Ham asked, "What did happen that night, Victor? The police picked you up from the lake after you ran away, not to mention five men went missing that night there too. I even hear that Steven was with you when all this happened."

"I wasn't running away. Me and Steven went to go put an end to something."

"What was that?"

"To put an end to the murders."

"What are you saying, you caught the killer?"

"We killed them."

"Killed them, you killed a man?"

"They weren't men, they were something else."

"Well then, what was it?"

Victor looked over from Ham to Keller and, with Steven by his side, he started to tell them the story. Whether or not they would believe him, he wasn't sure. "It was a werewolf, four of them."

Both Ham and Keller laughed when they heard, but Victor didn't seem to care, he just smiled.

"Well then, I'm sure you handled that pretty well, huh?" asked Ham, laughing.

Victor handed them the photo he took of the werewolf at the house.

"What's this?" asked Ham.

"Take a look," Victor replied.

Ham held the picture in both hands, with Keller looking over his shoulder. Keller looked at Victor and Steven and said, "It must be a fake."

"Well, I am not a make-up artist," said Steven.

"So, tell us how it all began," said Ham suspiciously.

Victor began to tell them the story, "Last week

when there was an attack at Ollie's, it was me who the werewolves were trying to hunt down because I walked onto their territory and they didn't like it. The old hermit, Willy, warned me about it but I went anyway because I wanted to know. So I went and that was the shit I brought back into town. Me and my family took refuge in Ollie's when they started coming after me. A clerk named Reggie was killed when they got in late in the night, and another man we could hear screaming outside. We tried to help him but it was too late. We managed to survive the night and killed two of them, while the other two retreated before sunrise. The following day, I refused to leave town and asked Steven to join me to hunt down the other two wolves."

"So you succeeded?" asked Ham.

"Yes."

"You expect us to believe that thing is real?" asked Keller, pointing at the photo.

"Don't really care," said Victor. He went on, "I have to be on my way. Talk to you guys later."

Victor made his way down the hall with Steven, and Victor said, "That Keller sure is a feisty one."

"Yeah, though some people do know it's better

not to piss him off. Keller is a brown belt and he can be quite aggressive when he fights."

"What can you tell me about Danny and Fuller?"

"Well, what you know about Danny is he's a joker and close to Fuller. They're on the soccer team together. Fuller, he's an extremely talented, all-round good athlete. Kind of a star and the school is his audience."

"Before we get to class, I have to ask. Are you coming to the funeral?"

"Are you kidding? After everything we've been through, I don't see why I should say no. I'm not sure about Ham and the others since they didn't know Willy. I mean, I didn't know him but it's worth it to go since I was beside you through all the trouble."

"I'm happy to hear that."

The two came to Socials where they met Ham, then decided they would sit together in class. Ham felt left out and unappreciated, and could see that for some reason Victor and Steven had become the best of friends.

Later that day in Photo class, Ham switched partners from Victor to Keller. Whether it was payback or not, Victor wasn't sure but Ham was now friends with Keller, although still friends with him.

At lunch, Victor went outside to sit on the bleachers with Steven and the rest. Both Danny and Fuller were practicing keep-ups with a soccer ball. Fuller was doing well and basically trying to show Danny how to do it. "Hey Ham, why don't you give us a tune with that horn you have. Maybe it will make me bounce the ball better."

Ham gave Danny the finger and Danny laughed saying, "Gee, is that the only note you know? Sorry, I thought you were like Hermann Baumann."

"So Victor, how long have you been in town?" asked Fuller.

"Less than two weeks."

"Ever played soccer?"

"I'm not too much of a sports person, although I did play soccer for two seasons when I was little."

"Why don't you try out for the team? The coach is always looking for more players."

Victor stood back, thinking about what Fuller said

and decided, "Yeah sure, why not. I usually have nothing better to do."

"That a boy!" said Fuller, delighted.

"Hey Fuller, I bet I can beat you in a race around the track," said Danny competitively.

"You know there's no way you're going to beat a track runner."

"Maybe, but at least I still do a lot around the field during the game."

"Well then, let's see. To the line!"

Danny and Fuller got to the starting line and were getting ready to sprint. Ham went down to signal them to go. "On your mark, get set, GO!!!"

The two sprinted down around the track. Danny was right beside Fuller each step but like Fuller said, Danny was no match for him once they came to 1200 m of the track. Danny became tired and twisted his ankle. Fuller kept on running, not knowing Danny was on the ground. Soon Danny picked himself up and limped the rest of the way. Fuller raced over the finish line, victorious. He looked back, smiling until he saw Danny trying to limp the rest of the way.

"What happened, did he sprain his ankle?" Fuller yelled up to the bleachers.

"Yeah, you didn't see?" asked Victor.

"No, I just kept running, thinking how much I wanted to make it back to the finish line. I just noticed when I stopped running."

Once Danny limped his way back he said, "Oh well, thanks for stopping, Jackie Kersee!"

"I'm sorry, I didn't notice. We were on heat out there and I didn't catch that."

"I need an ice pack. Can one of you run to get me one? I'm pretty sure we know the right man for the job…"

"Yeah, yeah sure, I'll go," said Fuller.

Fuller ran to the office to find an ice pack while Danny rested his ankle on the bleachers. "You do know Jackie Kersee is a woman, right?" asked Ham.

"Yeah whatever," said Danny. "I need to rest my ankle."

Danny pulled up his pant leg, took off his shoe and started to pull down his sock. Ham's eyes nearly popped out of his head saying, "What the fuck!"

"Dude, your ankle is so gross," said Keller.

"I'm in deep shit. How long does it take for something like this to heal? This means I can't play for a while."

Ham walked over on the bleachers above Danny and said, "Oh, don't worry, Daniel. You can always join band. I hear they're always looking for people who can play the Jew's harp."

"Yeah, really good joke, Ham," said Danny sarcastically.

"What? I just assumed that you were a Jew."

"Screw you!"

"Well, maybe if you weren't so cheap all the time and cared more about others rather than always trying to trick people to cover your expenditures."

"Since when have I done that?"

"This morning at the vending machine when you asked someone for a dollar, when of course you did have enough money in your pocket. I saw you take it out after he left."

"Well, you're obviously a Jew because your nose is in my business."

"You son of a…"

"Hey, come on you guys. I don't want to have to get Keller to stop you both. Would you want that?" Steven warned.

Soon after, Fuller brought Danny an ice pack and they all just chilled on the bleachers before next period. Before the bell rang, Danny's girlfriend, Fern, came out looking for him. She saw the dark blue and purple swelling on his ankle and said, "Are you okay? What happened?"

"Oh nothing. This asshole challenged me to a race around the track and for that I sprained my ankle."

"YOU challenged me to a race, Danny," said Fuller.

"Maybe we should go to the office and tell them you can't walk today," said Fern.

"Yeah let's go quickly, before the bell rings," said Danny.

As the two walked away, Danny hopping on one foot while Fern helped him with one arm around her shoulders, Victor asked, "So, who's that?"

"That is Danny's girlfriend, Fern. They've been together for over a year now. She was actually Ham's girl back in middle school."

"You're really going to bring that part up, Fuller?" asked Ham, irritated.

"Sorry, just thought he'd want to hear the whole story."

"Yeah well, let's just head to class. Break's almost over."

They all fanned out to their classes. Before Victor and Steven got to Cooking, they saw a student harassing another down the hall and Victor asked, "Who's that?"

"Don't mind him, that's Hector and he's a real bully."

The two walked into their classroom and started making hash browns. Ms. Unger was not in to teach, so they had a substitute cover, giving Ms. Unger time to herself to prepare for her husband's funeral. The sub didn't explain why she wasn't there, but of course Victor already knew.

After school ended, Ham again invited Victor to Ollie's, along with everyone else. Victor wanted to head home right away but thought he would stay maybe ten minutes at Ollie's. When they arrived, the six of them sat in two booths, deciding to have Slush Puppies while they talked. "So Victor, still thinking about joining the team?" inquired Fuller.

Victor took great thought and realized it would be worth doing since he's still a kid and in school, so he said, "Yes, I definitely will. I'm just wondering when would be the perfect time to come and join you."

"Come after school Monday. We're practicing and the coach will be happy to see you. We've already lost six players."

"Why is that?"

"Families have left since Alcoa shut down years ago. Since then the population has been becoming more… well, smaller."

"Why did it shut down?"

"Well, back in '78 there was an explosion at the plant. More than three hundred people died that day. A lot of families lives were affected greatly, but the real reason why so many people moved is because since they lost the plant, they lost their jobs. No one could find work here, so they needed to look elsewhere, ultimately pushing them to leave town."

"What caused the explosion?"

"They believe it was caused by a madman."

"What's his name?"

"His name was…"

"Ow! You stepped on my foot, you jackass," said Danny, infuriated.

"Sorry Danny, I thought your ankle was a foot stool," said Ham.

"Oh really, well…" Danny spits into Ham's French Horn, "sorry, I thought your horn was a spittoon."

"Oh, I guess that makes us even."

"I guess it does."

Victor saw Ollie and decided to go talk to him. "Hey Ollie, it's me, Victor. How are you?"

"Oh I'm good, Victor, how are you?"

"Great. You still coming to the funeral today?"

"Of course."

"Just checking. I can only imagine who will be coming since Willy lived a solitary life."

"Well in that case, there's someone I want you to meet."

Ollie yelled to a man in one of the aisles and said, "Hey Lou, could you come up to the till? There's someone I want you to meet."

As the man walked up, Ollie said, "Victor, this is Lou. He's an old friend of mine and Willie's. Three days ago I called him to invite him to the funeral."

"Nice to meet you," said Lou.

"Nice to meet you," said Victor. "Is there anyone else you know that's coming to the funeral?"

"Yes, a few more of our friends; Freddie and Tyrone, not to mention Willy's old girl, Tracy."

"So Lou, you from out of town?"

"Yes, I moved away a long time ago."

"Why, when?"

"About thirty years ago. After we lost one of our own."

"One of your own?"

"Yeah, Elmer. Back then we were all a gang. Willy, Freddie, Tyrone, Elmer, Ollie and me. There was this one night where Willy and Elmer framed this guy for assault, which sent him to prison."

Victor looked at them, distressed, and asked, "But why would Willy do that?"

"I guess because he could. The rest of us weren't part of it but when the man finally got out of prison he came after us. He shot Elmer when we broke into the school. He followed us there but Willy managed to stop him by killing him. Sometime after, the rest of us decided to turn Willy in, but we found out that Tracy had warned him and he left town. We believe he went to join the Army and we hadn't seen him since."

"I have," said Ollie. "Yeah, he came into my store years ago after returning from the war. He returned to be with Tracy but unfortunately she was with someone else and didn't have those feelings for him anymore. Since that time, I haven't seen him. I didn't even know he still lived here until Victor told me."

"You know… I used to feel bad for Willy but now hearing this, he's not worthy."

"Don't say that, Victor. You know, we might know things you didn't know about Willy, but something tells me you knew some things we didn't either."

"Well, I wouldn't know about that. You both make it really clear about who he really was. Now I don't even know what to say about him at his funeral."

"You believe what he lived and died for. Even I knew that there was good in that man, and if he was trying to help your family, then he deserves the right words given to him. I hated Willy but even enemies can show respect, and everyone deserves a proper burial so they can rest in peace."

"Ollie, you are a good and wise man and I thank you for comforting me because now I know what to say. Anyway, I should probably get going. I need to be ready for this afternoon and I guess the rest need to also."

"Yes, I'll be closing really soon so I can go to the

funeral, so you and your friends might want to leave soon."

"Alright, and thanks again, Ollie."

Ollie gave Victor a nod and, soon after, Victor and his friends left to go home.

When Victor got home, everyone was already dressed for the funeral so he went upstairs to put on his suit. When he came back downstairs, he asked his dad, "So, who will be coming?"

His dad only responded, "Just a few, not that I know their names." He asked Victor, "Where were you? I thought you'd be home earlier than this."

"Sorry, I stopped by Ollie's with my friends. I spoke to Ollie. He said he invited his old friends that knew Willy and they were going to be coming to the funeral."

"Oh, okay… Well, we should probably get going. The church is two blocks from your school and we have to drive into town."

Victor and his family made their way inside the church and found seats. Some people arrived after them, including some relatives of Willy's, but not many. Victor saw Steven and his mother enter, as well as Ollie and his friends.

A few minutes after the priest finished saying a few words about Willy and leading them in prayer, he asked if anyone wanted to come up to speak.

First Ollie went up to speak. He said, "Willy Snider was once a role model. Back then he was a friend and brother-like figure to me. I went most of my life without seeing him because he had sinned too much for me or any of his friends to have anything to do with him. But in a way, he was a good man, a visionary with ideas that… that Walt Disney would be proud of. I know that he was a loving man and he would have always cherished the woman he loved. He even had this old line about women. 'If you were holding two roses while looking in a mirror, you'd be looking at three of the most beautiful things in the world.' I know when he would make a promise to her, he would never break it and would do anything to be with her. So I know that he deserves this as much as the next man. And before you speak of anything else, I'd want you all to hear more about this man. I'd like to call up Victor Hyde… Victor."

Victor stood up and walked down the aisle to speak in front of everyone. Before speaking, he looked around the room, but what got his attention was Steven's mother, Tracy. Victor could see her crying and she seemed more devastated than anyone else in the room. What really made her cry was when Ollie mentioned how Willy would always cherish the ones he loved. She too remembered the line that Ollie mentioned, and noticed how Ollie looked at her when he told them about it. She began to feel regret, knowing she could have waited for Willy all those years ago but instead married someone else.

"I only knew Willy for a very short time. At first he was a total stranger to me but soon after he became like a guardian to me. And make no mistake… he was a hero. I believe he was a man of courage, integrity, but most of all, he was a man of great valor. I know because just a few days ago I found his Medal of Honor from when he served in the war. That's when I knew there was a lot more to that man than I had known before. He was a war hero that saved a lot of lives in Vietnam, and I'm sure those families would have wanted to thank him if they knew he was the reason their sons came home alive."

"What was really good was what he tried to do before he died. He tried to put an end to the abomination that was coming for me and my family, to put an end to it for what it had done to your families. Like a wise man once said, 'You can hate someone, but even enemies can show respect; they deserve a proper burial if they were trying to redeem themselves.' So I say this; Willy may be dead but his spirit lives on forever. And on this day he shall rest in peace, all thanks to his courage and the service he has done for others. To you, Willy, I say if you were still alive, anyone would have wanted to be your friend as you would make one of the best ones."

Within the hour, everyone had exited the church doors. When Victor and his family came out, an old man and four others walked up to speak to Victor. The old man approached Victor saying, "Hi, Victor. You don't know me but I just have to say I'm grateful for that speech you gave for Willy."

"Thanks," said Victor, shaking his hand. "What's your name?"

"My name is Jimmy."

"Jimmy, so how do you know Willy?"

"I know him because we fought side by side in the war."

"So wait, you mean you were in the same unit?"

"Yes, we were commanded by Willy in his own task force. Our old Lieutenant died and Willy took his place. His platoon became Willy's platoon. Willy was successful in all combat missions he fought, and I was always there to see it. We wouldn't have ever prevailed if it wasn't for him. So for that, I'd like you to meet the rest of the team."

The four others walked up to Jimmy and Victor, with Jimmy introducing them. "Victor, this Ian, Giuseppe, Dean and Fuller."

"Fuller? I too have a friend named Fuller."

They snickered at that comment and smiled at Victor, already knowing he was a good kid. "So, who told you about Willy's death?" asked Victor.

"Well, let's just say we have our ways of knowing when a fellow comrade has passed," said Jimmy, winking at Ollie.

"Well, I'm glad you all came and I'm more than grateful to meet the men that served with Willy."

"Thanks, Victor, and now that you're driving out to the cemetery, do you mind if we join you?"

"No, not at all. You all are more than welcome."

They all got into their cars and drove out to the cemetery to bury Willy. Victor, his family, Ollie, Lou, Freddie, Tyrone, Willy's old task force, and a few of Willy's relatives joined for the ride.

More tears fell as people got there, watching as Willy's body was lowered into the ground. Steven was nowhere to be seen; his mother decided to leave and go home since she couldn't stand to watch anymore. Finally, they all gave their last goodbyes and took off.

Before Victor and his family left, they saw more people in the cemetery carrying a casket to its grave. One person in the group was Victor's cooking teacher, Ms. Unger.

Victor pointed out, "I know that woman. That's my cooking teacher, Ms. Unger. Dad... I think I know why they're here. I need to go say something."

Victor looked over his shoulder at his dad, who gave Victor a nod. As the priest was praying for the deceased, Victor walked up behind Ms. Unger to pay his respects. Before the priest finished, Ms. Unger looked behind her, surprised to see Victor, but understood why he was there too.

"Hi, Ms. Unger."

"Hello, Victor."

"Look, I don't know if this means much but I just want to say I'm very sorry for your loss."

Ms. Unger dropped her head, looking over at her

husband's coffin, then looked back at Victor and said, "It's okay, Victor. I know everything and I'm glad you found the animal to avenge my husband's death." They hugged and Victor left, heading home.

In a week's time, the horror was past and everyone had gotten back on their feet to pick up where they started. Natalie quit her job and became a hairstylist like her father, while Susan became a cook at the restaurant in town. And Victor… well, finally he knew he had a place he could call home – a little town called Roarke.

About the Author

Kobi Madsen was born and raised in the beautiful, small town of Kitimat, British Columbia, Canada. From the young age of four, Kobi was diagnosed with Autism. Although he struggled in certain areas of his life, he made a choice to never let his diagnosis hold him back from any of his dreams. He recently graduated from Mount Elizabeth Secondary School. For as long as he can remember, he has had a strong interest in using his creativity, particularly in the performing arts industry. In 2013, he won Best Supporting Actor for his role as 'The Mysterious Man' in the production of *Into the Woods*. Ever since he was nine years old, after having a very realistic nightmare, he knew he wanted to begin writing a series of horror novels one day, and was inspired to write his first novel of the series, *Grimhunters*. He still resides in Kitimat, British Columbia, and is excited for what is to come. For now he enjoys traveling, spending time with his family, and is looking forward to attending university in the near future.